TAKE

A Collection of Submissive Adventures

mischief

Mischief
An imprint of HarperCollins*Publishers*
77–85 Fulham Palace Road,
Hammersmith, London W6 8JB

www.mischiefbooks.com

A Paperback Original 2013

First published in Great Britain in ebook format by
HarperCollins*Publishers* 2012

A catalogue record for this book is
available from the British Library

ISBN-13: 9780007553266

Set in Sabon by FMG using Atomik ePublisher from Easypress

Contents

Journey's End
Rose de Fer

Alice wakes, pale and shivering, her naked body exposed in the chilly morning light. She is still curled around his hand, his fingers deep inside her as he sleeps. For several minutes she lies perfectly still, watching dreams dance across his eyelids. His hand twitches slightly and her tiny gasp of pleasure makes him stir. Slowly his eyes open, meeting hers.

'You're cold,' he says. It is not a question.

He gently withdraws the hand that plumbed her depths so thoroughly the night before and she wriggles a little in protest, tensing her inner muscles as though she might trap his fingers there. He smiles indulgently as he draws the duvet up over her legs, leaving her upper body bare.

His warm wet fingers trace a line up her body, between her breasts and along the length of one thin arm, coming to rest where the ropes bind her wrists to the iron bedstead.

'Can you feel your hands?'

She is tempted to lie and tell him yes so he won't release her, but she knows he would see through any such dishonesty. Reluctantly, she shakes her head. When he unties the knots she lowers her arms with a hiss of pain as the pins and needles bring her achingly back to the real world. Her wrists are scored deeply where the ropes have bitten into her tender flesh throughout the night and he massages the skin as though smoothing away imperfections in a sculpture.

She moans as the blood flow returns and her legs twine about his, entreating him to stay. But, as always, he leaves with the light, abandoning her to her memories and the lingering pain. She hears the door close softly behind him and she lies in the tangle of sheets for more than an hour before dragging herself out of bed and into the shower.

✻ ✻ ✻

She met him on the train, on the way to a routine business meeting in London where she'd treated herself to a first-class ticket for a change. Free tea and a bit more leg-room made all the difference to what was usually a long, boring journey.

She'd been in his seat when he boarded the train and he hadn't said a word to her as she apologised and shifted clumsily over to the window, where her reservation was. His polite smile made her feel like a child forgiven some bit of mischief. He was well dressed, his dark suit immaculate and stylish, clearly hand-tailored. His face was chiselled and aristocratic, with eyes so deeply brown they were almost black. But it was his voice that really got her attention.

He was on the phone to someone, discussing his schedule in such vague terms that Alice couldn't guess what line of work he was in. But his voice! It was beautiful. Rich, silky and resonant. Like someone who read books aloud for a living. Or should do. She eavesdropped, pretending to read her cheap paperback as he confirmed details of a meeting in Soho the next day.

The firm authority in his voice made her squirm and she felt her cheeks growing warm as he sharply informed the person on the other end of the phone that something wasn't good enough, that they would have to do better.

Normally Alice hated the window seat. It made her feel trapped by whichever stranger got the aisle seat next to her. She loathed having to ask to be let out every time she needed the loo, which, with tea and the many hours between Edinburgh and London, was fairly often. The seats on the other side of the table were still vacant, although the reservation cards in the seat backs claimed that passengers would be boarding at Peterborough. In this case, however, she decided she didn't really mind feeling pinned in. Not by this man. She turned another page in her book and tried to keep her eyes on the page so as not to drool over him. She hadn't taken in a single word of the prose.

The man ended the call and tucked his phone away, breaking the spell of his voice. For a moment she basked in the echo of it before suddenly remembering that she hadn't told her boss what time she'd be getting in herself. She didn't want to ring him and replace her memory of the stranger's beautiful voice with Mr Carson's reedy whine so she decided just to send him a text. She reached into her bag for her phone and gave a small cry as a spike of pain flared in her middle finger.

Her companion looked up as she tentatively withdrew her hand. A jagged sliver of glass protruded from the fingertip. She stared at it with a mixture of horror and fascination, trying to imagine where it had come from. Blood was beginning to seep from the wound.

'Oh, dear,' the man said softly. He took her by the wrist and drew her hand towards him to peer closely at her finger. A strange smile flickered across his features. He gently plucked the shard of glass from her finger, making her wince with pain. But he didn't release her hand. Instead he grasped the injured finger and squeezed

it, causing a bead of blood to swell from the puncture.
Then he held her finger over his mug of tea. Transfixed,
Alice found herself unable to pull away.

One by one the crimson droplets fell into the cup and
dispersed in feathery swirls. The pressure he exerted made
her fingertip pulse, hot and stinging. The sensation ran
the length of her arm, burning a path along the network
of veins to her throbbing heart.

He released her hand then and her eyes widened even
more as he raised the cup to his lips and sipped from it,
his eyes never leaving hers.

Heat flared in her face at this unnatural intimacy.
She pressed a tissue to her finger, the skin still warm
from his touch. Unnerved, she glanced down at the table
and when she looked up again he was still watching
her. She opened her mouth to speak, but nothing came
out. She didn't know what to say anyway. In the man's
steady gaze was the supreme confidence that he was in
total control.

'Alice,' he said, as though pronouncing the name of
a delicacy.

Her heart fluttered at the sound of her name. 'Do I
know you?' she ventured at last.

He took her hand and peeled away the bloodstained
tissue to kiss her fingertip. 'Not yet.'

* * *

That had been almost two weeks ago. Alice had never reached her destination, nor let anyone know she wouldn't be coming. There was only Mr Carson, and she didn't really care if he fretted over her non-appearance. It wasn't like she was particularly vital anyway. Back home, of course, there was no one to miss her, not even a cat. When the train arrived at King's Cross her mysterious companion took her by the arm and led her along the platform to the taxi rank. He got in beside her and gave the driver the name of a hotel.

The suite he took her to was plush and elegant, so far removed from the Travelodge she'd been destined for that she might as well have been in another country. As she peered around the room she could feel the man watching her, studying her movements, drinking her in. There was no question that she was here for sex, but she had no idea whether he was waiting for some signal from her. She hadn't even asked his name. She hadn't dared to speak at all.

Finally he appeared behind her, making her jump. She closed her eyes as his hands encircled her, fitting neatly around her small waist before sliding up her body to cup her breasts. One gentle squeeze and then the hands were gone, leaving her breathless and wanting more. He lowered his mouth to her shoulder and her heart pounded wildly as he pulled the neck of her jumper open, exposing her collarbone.

6

Alice shivered in response to his warm, moist breath against her skin. She felt his tongue, then his teeth, biting gently. For one crazy moment she thought of vampires and when no fangs punctured her jugular she was genuinely surprised.

'Are you a good girl?' he asked in a seductive whisper.

The question startled her and it took her a moment to realise how much it also excited her. 'Yes,' she managed to say, her voice barely a voice at all.

'Are you going to do what I tell you to do?'

She shuddered. 'Yes.'

He kissed her throat again, released her and stepped away. He stood smiling at her. 'Take off your clothes.'

Although the command wasn't exactly unexpected, it still made her stomach flutter. Alice blushed fiercely and lowered her head. She felt self-conscious about her cheap high-street suit but she felt even more so about what was underneath. She couldn't remember the last time she'd undressed for a man but it had been a while.

Her fingers trembled as she unfastened the buttons of her jacket and slipped it off. He nodded towards a chair and she laid the jacket gently over one curled mahogany arm. Her blouse proved more of a challenge, the tiny buttons tripping up her nervous fingers. The man offered no assistance; he merely stood calmly by. Watching, waiting.

She unzipped her skirt and slipped it down over her

hips, wondering fretfully if he would like what he saw. But his lips parted in a smile as she stepped out of the skirt to reveal her girlish underwear. Flirty white cotton panties with a butterfly pattern and a matching bra. White lace-top holdups. She kicked off her low heels and then felt a sudden rush of panic at the thought of removing the rest. She kept herself in good shape but that hardly mattered; there wasn't a woman alive who wouldn't feel insecure in her position. However, the fear only paralysed her for a moment and she was reassured by the growing bulge in her companion's trousers.

'Alice,' he said, his voice edged with firmness.

Her knees trembled with fear and desire and she felt her sex moistening in response, just as it had on the train when she'd first heard his voice. Quickly, so as not to lose her nerve, she reached behind to unhook her bra and slipped it off, exposing her breasts. She stepped out of her panties and tossed them onto the chair with the rest of her clothes. The riot of butterflies looked out of place in the elegant room, like childhood fairies that had lost their way and suddenly found themselves in the scary grown-up world.

Swallowing her fear, Alice peeled off her holdups before she had to be told. Her legs tingled as they were released from the constricting nylon and she curled her toes into the soft pile of the carpet, hoping he wouldn't notice the chipped polish. Out of the corner of her eye she caught a glimpse of herself in a full-length mirror, standing naked before this stranger. It was all she could do to resist the urge to cover herself but she was too frightened of his disapproval. She didn't know what to do with her hands. They hung by her sides, her fingers plucking nervously at the gooseflesh on her thighs.

'Are you cold?'

She shook her head. Just nervous, she thought but didn't say. It wasn't necessary; he could see she was terrified. He also seemed to be relishing her fear.

'Hold out your hands,' he said.

She obeyed at once, both the command and her instant compliance sending hot little pulses through her body.

When she saw the ropes she gasped and took one hesitant step back, but she didn't lower her hands. She saw his eyes register her moment of fright and then his lips curled in a smile that was both sexy and sinister. His erection grew.

'I asked you if you were a good girl, Alice, and you told me you were.'

Her face burned at the gentle chastisement. She swallowed audibly. 'I am,' she said in a voice that was barely a whisper. 'I'm sorry.'

'I'm sorry what?'

Blood rushed so violently to her head that for a moment she thought she might faint. 'I'm sorry, sir.'

'That's better.'

He pushed her wrists together and then wrapped the coil of rope around them. Tight enough to hold without being painful. He knotted the rope and then wound the free ends up between her wrists, tying them off to create a pair of coiled manacles.

Alice didn't need to test whether they would hold her. She wouldn't have tried to escape for anything. There was no question of his control. Her sex was throbbing so intensely it was almost painful.

The man led her to the bed and Alice followed like an obedient puppy on a lead. All her senses felt heightened, overwhelmed. She caught the scent of his cologne, something spicy and mysterious. It mingled with the polished wood of the furniture and the sharp smell of the wrought-iron bedstead. She imagined she could still smell the blood from her finger, the blood he had tasted.

When he lifted her and set her down on the bed she sagged with relief. She didn't think her legs could have supported her much longer.

He withdrew another length of rope from his pocket and watched her expectantly. Alice writhed against the velvety duvet, understanding the silent instruction. She raised her arms above her head and he smiled his approval as he bound her wrists to the cold iron of the bedstead. Then he slowly circled the bed like a predator, looking down at her from every angle.

It was only after he was satisfied that he began to

undress himself. He took his time removing his jacket, his shirt, his trousers and, finally, his underpants. Alice watched, spellbound, as bit by bit he revealed his lean, athletic body, his broad chest and muscular thighs. When his cock sprang free at last she began to tremble uncontrollably. Tears blurred her vision and a lump formed in her throat.

She was baffled by her response. She wanted him desperately. She'd been attracted to him from the very first moment. Now she was here, stripped and bound in his hotel room, and he was about to fuck her. She was exhilarated and frightened and she could feel her sex dampening with nearly unbearable desire. Why on earth was she crying?

Her companion was eyeing her curiously, as though amused by her emotional display. At last he sat beside her and placed one warm hand against her chest.

'I can feel your little hummingbird heart,' he said softly. 'Are you really so afraid?'

'Not afraid,' she managed to choke out, 'it's just … I don't know. It's …'

'Intense?'

She nodded, grateful to him for supplying the word for her. 'Very intense. I've never –'

He stopped her words with a kiss and she melted into the taste of him. His tongue entered her mouth, warm and velvety. When he drew away at last, she was calmer.

Her heart no longer felt like it would leap from her chest and her trembling had subsided. Now she merely felt foolish, like a child unprepared for grown-up games.

He leaned his head down to her ear and whispered, 'Let go.'

She swallowed the lump in her throat and nodded, eager to obey, eager to be taken wherever he would take her.

'Was that a yes?'

'Yes,' she echoed, her voice a hoarse croak. And when his brow furrowed slightly she added, 'sir.'

'Good girl.'

He kissed her again and she closed her eyes. Every show of dominance made her sex throb with longing. And now, as his hands began to explore her naked flesh, she gave herself over to him completely. She was his. His to use as he saw fit, his to play with however he wished.

She moaned as he kneaded her breasts, tweaking the nipples into stiffness before placing tingling little kisses on them. He drew his fingers down the length of her body and she writhed as he gently parted her thighs. A flush of embarrassment burned her face as he peered closely at her, inspecting her. For a moment she became fretful, wondering whether she had shaved closely enough, whether he was pleased with what he saw, wondering how she must measure up to others. Then he touched her and banished all her worries.

His fingers stroked her plump pink lips, slipping easily over their eager wetness before entering her. She gasped and threw back her head, straining against the ropes. The expert knots made her feel both trapped and secure. She wasn't going anywhere; she *couldn't*. He could do anything he liked to her and even if she could have resisted, she knew she wouldn't. His absolute control freed her from both guilt and responsibility.

Her hips seemed to move independently as he pushed his fingers deep inside. She clenched around him, urging him deeper, begging him with her body for more. When he manipulated her cervix she whimpered softly at the strange sensation but she didn't want him to stop. To her surprise she realised that she wanted even more. She wanted him to penetrate her so roughly and deeply that she would feel it for days. She wanted the ropes so tight her hands went numb.

It was almost impossible to believe she was here like this, burning with hunger for this dark stranger. It wasn't like her at all. She had never been a particularly passionate lover; nor was she what anyone would call reckless. But this man had awakened something in her. Something lustful and primal and yet shockingly submissive.

An image sprang into her mind then. She saw herself kneeling naked at his feet, her face resting lovingly against his polished black boot, her back scored with welts from a lash, her hip branded with his initials. His slave. His plaything. His property to do with however he saw fit. The strange fantasy startled her as much as it excited her and she moaned hungrily as she pushed her hips forward, a wordless plea for him to take her, fuck her. She had never felt so aroused in her life.

At last he withdrew his fingers and positioned himself above her. She met his eyes and her breath caught in her throat. It was finally going to happen. Without prompting she murmured a single word and felt his cock harden even more against her sex.

'Master.'

She expected him to enter her in a single violent thrust but he surprised her again by taking his time. His eyes gleamed with sensuous cruelty as he made her wait, teasing her by putting himself in a bit at a time, inch by slow inch.

Alice had never known such overwhelming desire, had never even known it was possible. Without the ropes she would have been clutching him, driving him deeper inside her, demanding that he fuck her harder. But he was the one in control and it was more intoxicating than anything she had ever experienced.

After what seemed an eternity of teasing he finally buried himself inside her, slamming into her and making her cry out with complete abandon. His powerful thrusts awakened every nerve in her body and she thrashed in her bonds, further stimulated by the knowledge that she couldn't escape. She hooked her legs around his, pressing herself as tightly into him as she could while he filled her, engulfed her, transported her.

Soon she was screaming, with no thought about who might hear her. Nothing mattered but this moment and the incredible pleasure she had never dreamed possible. She yanked at the ropes to heighten the sensation of helplessness as she drowned in the waves of a devastating climax.

His own followed soon after and he growled her name as he stiffened and quivered and emptied himself into her.

Afterwards they both slept, but he did not untie the ropes.

* * *

Her bondage became a ritual. Days passed and she found she couldn't sleep without being tied. If she needed the toilet in the night she had to wake him so he could untie her. As soon as she was done he restrained her again.

Sometimes he woke her in the night to fuck her and sometimes she would lie awake hoping he would. She would turn onto her side and angle her bottom against him, writhing against his cock until she felt it harden. Sometimes he indulged her, sometimes not.

She never dared to ask his name. He was only 'Master'.

And each night she gave herself to him, completely and utterly.

* * *

Alice blinks herself awake as the spray of the shower draws her reluctantly out of her memories. She feels his absence like a wound, one that only heals while he is with her and reopens each time he leaves. The hot water burns where her skin has been bruised or scratched and she imagines that he is here, washing her clean so that he may dirty her again. Her body is his canvas.

Her soapy hands stray down between her legs, but her fingers can never make her feel the way his do. His seem capable of tearing her apart.

She is reminded of the night he piled the pillows up in the middle of the bed and draped a towel over them. He had tied her arms in front and spread her buttocks. She moaned with the delicious sense of shame as he lubricated the tight opening of her arse and then took her. A virgin there, Alice had bled. Afterwards she felt reborn. She was sore for days but the pain had been a comfort to her while he was away, a reminder of his touch, of his complete ownership of her.

She has no idea where he goes during the day or what he does. He leaves her each morning with instructions not to go anywhere. She is allowed to sit in the hotel lobby while the maid makes up the room but she must return once it is done. She is not to watch the news or read the paper.

Time has lost its meaning for her. There is only the night, when she is alive, and the awful aching yearning during the day when he is gone.

Occasionally it occurs to her to wonder at his secrecy. He might be a criminal for all she knows. A gangster or a serial killer. But the thought is strangely abstract, something so far removed from the bliss of her cloistered existence that it has no relevance to her at all.

She steps out of the shower and dries herself, gingerly patting her small injuries, the little cuts and bruises that prove to her she isn't dreaming. She cherishes each one. When she is dry she puts on the fluffy hotel robe and makes herself a cup of tea. Each sip reminds her how he first tasted her blood on the train. Her sex pulses in response as she curls up in the chair by the window.

Outside are the vibrant, noisy streets of London. She sees the endless stream of traffic. People, taxis, big red buses. Everyone has somewhere to go, somewhere to be. Destinations, appointments, assignations. But the bustle may as well be on another planet for all it affects Alice. Her world is here, in this room. When her master is here, she is his. And when he is gone, she waits. That is all she knows, all she wants to know.

Shattered
Sommer Marsden

I stared at it, trying not to feel discouraged. The fixer-upper I had bought and proceeded to gut was coming along much, much slower than I'd thought. My tiny deck outside the small kitchen was a mess. It was only about eight by six. Built as an offshoot where a backdoor should have been, it stood on what must have been twenty-foot stilts, suspending the deck above the yard below.

'Not what I was hoping for,' I sighed. I'd stopped in to check on the work. Oddly, of the entire house I'd bought, it was this tiny odd little porch I was most excited about.

'We'll get it there.'

I jumped about a foot, clutching my heart and making an ungodly noise. Anger rushed through me in a red wave at being startled *and* embarrassed.

'What. The. Hell?' I ground out.

Then I was face to face with him and he grinned. 'Sorry. I thought you'd hear me clumping in here in these clodhoppers.' He pointed to his thick and dusty work boots. Steel-toed, no doubt.

'I didn't.' Now I was ashamed of my temper. 'I was lost in the world of dream home makeovers.'

He laughed. My stomach tumbled at realising it was *him*. The one and only worker on my disastrous and constantly shifting home project that I had noticed. More than once I'd felt the tickle of energy on my skin and turned to see him staring at me. More than once I had found myself staring at him and then been caught red-handed when he'd turned and spotted me.

And we'd smile and look away. Me with a blush. Him barking orders at men.

'We're getting there. Don't worry.'

'Not as fast as I hoped.' I stopped looking at him because it was starting to get hot in the kitchen even with the door to the deck open.

'These things never go as fast as we hope,' he said.

I turned fast and didn't stop myself. 'What's your name? Mine is Maggie. I know you know that but I don't know ... yours.'

'John. John Frost.'

I nodded. 'Nice to –'

He took two big steps toward me. The motion both comforting and aggressive – a looming, sexy oxymoron.

'– meet you,' I gasped.

When he reached out to touch me, I never questioned it. When he turned me back to face the porch, his large body crowding mine but not actually touching me, I never complained. 'What will it be, Maggie?' he asked me.

His breath was hot in my ear and I could barely hear his words because my head was full of the sound of my almost violent heartbeat. My top lip beaded with a fine cool sweat and I could feel my hands shaking, so I clenched them into fists. 'A bed, mostly.'

Laughter rumbled out of him and shook his body, which in turn shook me. 'A bed?'

I nodded, smiling. 'A bed,' I echoed. All of my effort was focused on not focusing on the fact that my body felt tingly and electric where he was touching me.

He leaned in closer. His bulk almost but not quite touching mine. His fingers curled more firmly to my shoulders and my nipples peaked as easy as you please. I wondered if John Frost could see over my shoulder and make out the shamefully plain evidence of what he was doing to me.

'I want it to be new hardwood and a bed that rests up against the back wall. Layers and layers of colourful fabric. Like gypsy fabric, but a big fat tall bed fit for a princess. Like a daybed on steroids.'

'A gypsy princess?' he asked. When his lips came down on the back of my neck a small strangled cry slipped out of me. His fingers bit into my shoulder again and I held my breath until spots appeared.

Is this what all our shared looks and unaddressed attraction had done? And did I want this to go forward?

I exhaled, hearing the shiver in my breath. Then inhaled deeply like I was doing yoga and I had my answer. Yes. This was what I wanted. We were the only ones here and I'd been fixated on this tall, bulky, blond man for ages. His eyes were the colour of seawater and the scar that ran through his left eyebrow never failed to make my pussy wet.

'A gypsy princess,' I stammered.

'What do you want to do on this bed, Miss Maggie?' He stopped kissing me but his hands slid around my waist and splayed, and his palms rested over my waistband. His fingers pointed down and brushed the top of my sex. My clit thumped along with my pounding heart. I was so wet between my legs I might be embarrassed if I didn't want him so badly.

I wished my gypsy bed was out there. Layers and layers of thick padding and bright fabric. Because I'd want him to fuck me on it. Out in the cool night air under the navy-blue sky, pinpricked with white stars.

'What would you do on this bed?' He unsnapped my pants. One snap, two snap ... and then he put his hands under my blouse. Not high up, just along the stripe of skin above my waistband. I made a mewing sound so full of need my cheeks blazed with shame.

'I would read.'

'And?' Those hands slipped a bit higher. Cool night air rushed in through the dilapidated screen door and licked at my exposed skin.

'And sleep.'

'And?' Higher still. Brushing along my ribcage so that my skin pebbled up in gooseflesh. My body was simultaneously hot and cold, light and heavy.

My breath shivered just like my body and I said, 'And … other things.'

I felt him smile against my hair and his fingers tickled up along my skin and cupped my breasts. He was brave and I was willing. 'Would those other things be … maybe … fucking?' When he said that, John pinched my nipples hard through my sheer bra.

My body jolted as if filled with an electric current and he took that moment to press himself against the back of me. I could feel his cock, hard and impressive, riding the split of my bottom. 'You know, boss lady, I've been watching you for quite a while.'

I swallowed convulsively, trying to keep my wits about me. He was scrambling my brain. Touching me, kissing my neck, rubbing himself against my willing form. 'I know.'

He chuckled. 'Do you?'

'I do, because ...' His warm, rough hands pushed up under my bra, forcing it out of the way, and cupped my now naked tits.

'Because?'

'I've been watching you back,' I finished. Time to be brave back, Maggie, I scolded myself. Because, under all my nervousness, I wanted this. Very much.

'Oh, really?' But we both knew he was aware. He walked me forward to the screen door that looked out onto the barely illuminated square of my wrecked deck.

Who knew who was watching? Who knows who could see us?

It was all irrelevant, though, because I was trapped between his big strong arms and he was sliding his hands down my sides, stroking my belly, pushing his long fingers under my waistband and into my panties. One fingertip found my clit and I grew tense in his arms from the sudden friction.

'Shh-shh-shh, boss lady,' he said. I stilled, going soft in his embrace. My head rested against his shoulder and I felt the bunch and dance of his biceps moving as he manipulated his fingers lower and slid one into me. John curled that finger just so and I heard myself purr in response.

We were utterly silent, the outside chatter of the city filtering through the fine screen door. I was close enough to the door that if I stuck my tongue out, I'd be touching it. He wanted me to see out, or he wanted someone to see in. A thrill shimmered in my gut and I gasped when he drove a second finger into my cunt and flexed his fingers again.

'See, if you had that bed, I'd start with this. I'd get you on that bed and trap you against me and I'd fuck you with my fingers until you gave it up for me. A sweet little orgasm where I could feel your pussy spasm around my hand and watch your face when you came.'

Despite the cool air from the door, I felt like I was suffocating. There wasn't enough air – or I couldn't get it fast enough as he shoved a third finger in and curled the bundle to my tender inside flesh.

'I never –' I started but then my words turned into a long exhalation as he pushed just a bit deeper and his palm banged against my clitoris.

'Never what?'

I shook my head as he moved a little faster, a little rougher now that I was so damn wet.

'Never what?' he asked again as my body gave that first greedy clench of an approaching peak. That first tight grip of an orgasm on the way.

'I never come this way,' I groaned, sagging in his arms shamelessly as I did just that. My pussy rippling and milking at his thrusting fingers until I was shaking as if I had a fever.

'That was a pretty strong never,' he said. He shoved

my jeans down to my knees and then bent to push them lower. My panties got dragged along with them and I found myself bare from the waist down in the torn-apart kitchen of my future home. Facing a screen door that was nothing but a tall spying window for the darkened city.

He pushed me forward and I went. His tented fingers shoved the squeaky old door open and we were out on the deck. It sort of groaned when our weight hit it and I yelped. 'What is that?'

'That is dry rot,' he said, moving me so that I stood where my future gypsy bed would be.

'Oh my God, go in. We're going to die.'

'We're not going to die,' John said, turning me towards the whitewashed wall. He put my palms up on the wall and pressed against me again. My heart was a palpable thing in my temples, banging away like it needed to escape. His zipper was loud to me even over the night sounds and I felt the hot bare skin of his cock run from the small of my back down the crack of my ass and back up again.

He shifted his sizeable bulk and the porch creaked. 'I can see the ground through some of the boards,' I wheezed. I was scared, but I was also excited.

The thought of him fucking me here was beyond a turn-on. The thought of us plummeting to our deaths … not so much.

He pressed himself against me and reached around

to grab my breasts. He pinched and squeezed with the perfect amount of chaotic pressure to leave me breathless. We'd been dancing around each other for what felt like ages. Glances and smiles, but sometimes just ignoring each other because we weren't supposed to go there. So when he trapped my nipples tight between his fingers, I sighed long and lusty.

'Tell me no and we can be done. Consider that hand-induced orgasm a gift, on the house.'

I didn't let my mind pick at the problem. I pushed back from the wall and turned fast. He gave me slack to let me move, probably assuming I was backing out. Instead, I grabbed his face in my hands and stood on tiptoe. Something cracked and I whimpered, but just kept kissing him. I found his cock with my hand and circled my finger around him, squeezing so that *he* made a desperate noise this time.

'I don't want to change my mind. I'm in. I'm scared we're going to crash and die but I'm also scared to miss this chance.'

His fingers dipped into me again as if it were a test. Finding me still soaked, he grunted with pleasure. 'Stay right here.'

And there I stood, hands wrestling each other nervously as I waited. The city whispered around me, bright lights from the harbour just a mile away as the crow flies, winking merrily. I scanned the windows to see if any of my neighbours might be spying on my current state of confused undress.

He came back, the porch shuddering as his weight hit it. He held an ice chest. When he motioned with his head for me to move, I scuttled towards the house instead of the outer rail. That way, when the whole dry-rotten mess came tumbling down I could dive madly for the door.

'Live and laugh, and fuck on the edge of danger,' he said, chuckling. But then, 'I'm only kidding. I promise you it will hold.'

I wasn't sure what emotion was winning the war in my chest at the moment. My yammering anxiety or my shouting arousal. He patted the ice chest and said, 'Sit.'

'I –'

'It's a bit short,' he said, encircling my wrist with his thick fingers and moving me when I remained frozen. 'But we can pretend it's your gypsy bed. And I can show you what I'd like to do to you, boss lady.'

'How long?' I blurted.

He put my hand on his cock and said, 'Well, I'd like to say about nine –'

A high, manic burble came out of me and then I snorted. Dear God. 'Not that,' I said. 'How long have you been … interested?'

'That's what you want to know?' He cocked his head when he said it and it gave him an endearing quality. He pushed me gently with just his fingertips and I sat down a bit too hard on the ice chest. I heard bits of old wood break free from under the porch and fall to the yard. The whole deck was shattered. Just like my nerves.

My heart rate picked up speed again but I noticed the steady wet thump in my cunt was almost unbearably pleasant. As scared as I was.

'Yes. That's what I want to know.'

He got on his knees in front of me, taking his own sweet time. He nudged my thighs apart. The streetlight from below lit the right side of his face a cool blue, while the light from the kitchen lit the left a warm yellow. He was an angel, a demon, a new lover I'd fantasised about.

'Since day one,' he said, lowering his mouth to my navel, kissing me so that I wanted to shiver and shift, but then the deck creaked and I was too afraid. 'In fact, one night I got off not once but twice, just thinking about kissing you for hours.'

'Oh,' I said as he kissed lower. And then 'Oh' again as his mouth settled on my pussy. He sucked my outer lips one at a time in a slow and deliberate way and when he finally slipped his tongue into my wet folds and found me at my centre, I gripped the hard plastic lid of the ice chest with shaking fingers.

John put his fingers in me again, curling slow, making me beg with small subtle thrusts of my hips. He sucked my clitoris, making the small muscles in my abdomen flutter and dance.

'Is it that important?'

'Yes. No ... Yes.'

He chuckled, hot breath rushing over my sex. 'Make up your mind, Miss Maggie.'

'No,' I finally decided.

'And you?' He licked long wet stripes over my flesh and paused every so often to press the flat of his tongue to the hard knot of my clit. The moment my body would go slack, he'd give me a wet circle or swirl or suckle so that I'd go tense again.

'Me what?' I gasped, finally remembering his question.

'How long – if at all – were you interested in me?'

'From the moment I saw you,' I said. No point in lying.

He gave a single nod as if to say, *That's settled* ...

'Now back to this imaginary bed,' he said.

I was enraptured by his eyes in this light. And his voice. And the steady thrum of my body in response to what he was doing.

'Yes, my gypsy bed. Layers and layers of bright fabric and yummy cushioning.'

'Exactly. See, I can picture you out here, in the twilight, a glass of wine or iced tea.' As he spoke he ran the head of his dick from my clit to my wet opening. Then a bit farther back. Only to drag it all the way back up through my moisture. When he teased my clitoris with his wet tip, my body shuddered and again the porch groaned. I grabbed his biceps, white-knuckling it.

29

'Hey now, would I be out here with you if I thought we were –'

'Going to die?' I blurted.

'In danger,' he said and grunted. His cock made that wet journey again and I forgot to be afraid again.

'Wine,' I said.

'What?'

'It would be wine. I'd have.'

'Ah yes, wine,' he said, slipping just the tip of himself in me and staying that way. Stretching that ring of muscle, making my pussy want to draw him in and clamp down on him. Instead I tried to breathe and hold on. 'And then, as I was saying, I'd find you there with your wine.'

A kiss on my belly as he curved his back. And yet he did not move his hips. He did not drive into me.

'I'd find you with your wine and I'd do what I just did. Part those pretty white thighs and eat your pussy. Until you came. And then, pretty lady, I'd put myself between those thighs ...'

Still he didn't move. And I couldn't breathe. My cunt clenched, trying to get more friction, failing.

'And I'd fuck you until you said my name. More than once.'

'Please,' I said.

'Please what?'

'Please don't torture me,' I said with a laugh.

'Like this?' He slipped into me fully, filling and

stretching me and finally, blissfully, kissing me. I grasped his face and let him bully my mouth with his even as he moved.

The porch groaned, some dead wood fell, my eyes flew open and I saw again the pinpoint dots of holes in the wood, backlit by the street lamps.

'Shh,' he said, gripping my hips hard and thrusting into me. 'We're fine. I promise.'

I wrapped my leg around his waist and tugged him to me even as he moved that way anyway. Long and thick, he touched nerve endings in me that were long dormant and very greedy. A thick rush of warm pleasure filled my pelvis and I groaned.

'We won't fall,' he said.

'It's not that,' I whispered, dragging my hands down his big arms, over his broad back, only to plunge them back into his short wheat-coloured hair.

'Then what?

'You're big.'

He laughed.

'And thick.'

This time he was silent and his breathing went harsh.

'And perfect,' I said.

John Frost thrust hard and his pelvic bone smacked my swollen clit and I came. I didn't expect it, I was swimming in a viscous syrup of pleasure, but that extra startling stimulation drove me over the edge.

He stilled. 'Christ.'

'What? What?' I babbled as my body continued to milk out every delicious drop of bliss.

'I don't want to come yet,' he said, kissing my nipple, my collar bone, my chest. He stayed still, no doubt to stave off his orgasm.

I pushed my palms against the ice chest and he moved back when I tried to stand.

'Where you going?'

'Losing my mind.' I leaned forward briefly, seeing the edges of the deck where the wood was the most shattered. The thin places that were the most dangerous. I licked the tip of his cock for a moment, just to hear him shift, just to hear him groan. 'Come on,' I said.

Was I really going to do this? Had I utterly lost my mind?

'What is it they say about adrenalin and fucking?' I asked myself more than John.

But he heard me and chuckled. 'It's not nearly as dangerous as you think it is.'

I put my hand on the railing, my body licked by cool night air. I pushed the old wood just enough that it rocked. It creaked and I whispered, 'Really?'

'Really. Wood and nails are sturdier fare than you think.' He'd moved up behind me, pressing his cock to the split of my ass.

I hummed and arched back against him. 'Do it,' I said.

John chuckled, but a big possessive hand fanned my

lower back, making my nipples grow harder still. He stroked the ladder of my spine, ticking off each vertebra with the tip of his fingers. 'Are you sure about that, Maggie? You're so scared you're shaking and yet you want me to fuck you while you brace against it?'

'I've been scared for ever. Part of dealing with it was buying this house and now part of it that I want is this … freedom. To be wild and alive and not afraid of falling.'

He pushed my thighs wider and slid the tip of his cock along me until he found my wet split. He held my hips as I gripped the railing, then thrust into me. My body rocked forward, pushing me onto my toes, forcing my weight forward so the railing groaned. I shivered but my pussy clenched up tight around him. So tight that he noticed. 'Fuck,' he growled.

I pushed back, ratcheting up the friction between us. Bracing myself with one hand, feeling the railing rock some but ignoring it even as the adrenalin spiked through me, I found my clit and started to rub. The grip of his hands on me, the cadence of his breath, all said he was close. And I was close, the fear as blissful as the pleasure.

John looped his big arm around my waist, bringing his body closer to me. His thrusts were deep and hard and when I rubbed my clit my body bloomed with heat and delight.

'Hang on, boss lady,' he growled and thrust harder. Once, fast and brutal.

I rocked against the railing and wood cracked dryly. Shards fell away and, seeing it all come undone, I came undone too. Coming hard, rippling around his still-driving cock. He laughed, but it was a wild laugh like one born of an adrenalin rush. Taking a step back from the edge as the far left corner of the rail toppled over, I heard it hit the yard below with a dull thud.

'You're a walk on the wild side,' he said. 'First you're terrified … then you're ready for cliff diving, so to speak.'

He pulled free of me and I turned, rushed at him, drove him back as I moved forward. When we hit the safety of the kitchen, I jumped against him hard and kissed him. We both went down in a heap on the old kitchen tiles. He grabbed my hair, looping his hand in a tangle of it, and hauled me in for another kiss.

'That was … that was … wow!' I laughed. My hand found his cock and I was stroking him again. He was growing hard already.

'Yeah, imagine the things I'm going to do to you when that gypsy princess bed is out there.'

I straddled him and ground my wet pussy on his pubic bone. I felt the rise and press of his growing erection against the cleft of my ass. Adrenalin, apparently, did do amazing things for a body.

His hands slipped under my top and found my breasts. Pinching, kneading, squeezing me until I shut my eyes and let my head fall forward. 'So …' I said, trailing off.

He put his hand to my mouth and covered my lips. My pulse spiked when he did it. Just like the railing and the fucking on the dilapidated porch, it held the potential for danger. His hand was big, my mouth was small. He caught the look in my eye and moved his hand down to circle my neck. When he pressed his thumb and pinky to the pound of my pulse, I grew wetter.

'So ... I figure that this deck, this bed, this gypsy project should become my focus. My personal project.'

I rocked against him, watching those ice-blue eyes darken a shade with arousal.

'Yeah?'

'Yeah,' he said. 'And then when my crew leaves for the day maybe you could come check out my progress. Make sure it's good.' He squeezed my neck softly so that my head felt muffled and fuzzy for a split second. Then he released me and reeled me in with a lock of hair.

He kissed me, then waited for me to speak.

'Yeah,' I agreed. I found him with my hand and put him back to my wet entrance. Before I sank down I said softly, 'I'll bring the wine.'

Spank It Out
Heather Towne

Julie had known Vincent since high school. They regularly
got together for lunch, talked on the phone, exchanged
e-mails. Vincent was a mild-mannered accountant, soft-
spoken, with neatly combed brown hair and a somewhat
bland face. He seldom got upset about anything. That's
why it surprised Julie so much when they met at a
restaurant one Friday noon, and Vincent seemed about
ready to burst into tears.

'What's wrong, Vincent? I've never –'

'It's Cassie!' the normally self-controlled man blurted
out for the entire restaurant to hear. 'I–I think she's
cheating on me!'

Julie glanced around at the alarmed patrons, then
reached across the table and patted Vincent's hand, trying
to calm her friend down. Although she wasn't the least
bit surprised to hear this news; she'd figured it'd been

coming for a long time, as long as Vincent and Cassie had been married. Two years.

Cassie was a buxom blonde with a bubbly personality and boisterous attitude, almost the exact opposite of her staid, timid husband, outgoing and outspoken. It had always seemed odd to Julie that the pair had ever even found each other, let alone married; an extreme example of opposites attracting. They'd seemed to make it work, however; up to now, anyway.

'What makes you think Cassie's cheating on you, Vincent?' Julie calmly asked. As a police officer, she was skilled at handling distraught civilians.

Vincent looked down at the tablecloth, his small, pale hand shaking under Julie's slender one. 'Once a week, regularly, she goes out at night – late at night.' His brown eyes behind the lenses of his glasses glistened. 'She thinks I don't hear her, but I do. She goes somewhere – I don't know where – and then comes back a couple of hours later, early in the morning …'

Julie's large blue eyes reflected sympathy. She asked the question, though she could guess the answer. 'Have you asked her – where she goes, what she does?'

Vincent's whole body shook. 'No! I can't!' he bleated. 'It's … I'm afraid of the answer. I know I'm not good enough for her, never was!'

Julie gripped his hand. 'Now, Vincent –'

'No, it's true!' Vincent gritted his teeth, staring

desperately at Julie. 'But I have to know. I have to be sure.'

The waiter drifted over. Julie shooed him away with her free hand. 'Well, you're just going to have to confront her, demand to know what's going on. Maybe it's not so bad ...'

'I want you to find out, Julie! You're a detective. At least, a police officer, I mean. You're skilled at this kind of thing.'

Julie opened her mouth to try to dissuade the man, but he kept on talking, letting it all out. 'She's always so tired afterwards, sore, and so quiet and subdued. It's like she's a completely different person, for a day or two. She's so nice to me then that–that I can't come out and ask her. But you can find out for sure – find the evidence of what she's up to.'

Julie steeled herself for the next question, which had to be asked. She'd been dragged in this far, she might as well go all the way. 'Do you two still have sex, Vincent?'

The man gulped. 'Not for a few days after she's ... been out. But afterwards, yes, in the dark, in our usual ...'

Julie smiled. 'You can tell me, Vincent. Friend to friend.' She was about to add, 'Victim to law officer', but bit her tongue in time.

Vincent flushed, then shrugged. 'Well, uh, we do our usual thing – missionary position, I, uh, guess they call it. Cassie used to try to get me to experiment with other

positions, but now she seems content with just that …
every now and then.'

'Uh-huh.'

'Follow her, Julie. Find out what's going on. I have
to know!'

Julie squeezed Vincent's hand. She'd never seen her
friend so passionate about anything before, and she
knew, as a friend, she had to help. 'OK, Vincent, if
that's what you really want. I'm working day shifts
this week, so I'll stake out your house at night, find
out what I can. But you're probably not going to like
what I find out.'

Some relief showed in Vincent's eyes, and he smiled
weakly. 'Thanks, Julie. I have to know. Maybe I can still
do something – to save our marriage.'

* * *

Julie parked three houses down from Vincent and Cassie's
modest bungalow that night, pulling up around eleven
o'clock. Her black sedan with the tinted windows was
inconspicuous, just another car in line on the quiet street.
Most of the houses, including the one at 315, were
already darkened. Julie sipped a cup of cold coffee, played
Minesweeper on her mobile phone.

At 12.21, the front door of the bungalow opened.
Someone slipped out into the shadows. Low-hanging

clouds covered the moon, but in the dim light shed by the widely-spaced streetlights Julie's trained eye could see that the person was wearing a headscarf and trenchcoat, and clutching a purse. And in the stillness of the night, she could hear the white high heels click-clacking hurriedly down the sidewalk, running away from the home, white-stockinged legs flashing in the yellow light. The front and back of the shapeless trenchcoat were packed tight with hot-blooded woman.

There was a cab waiting at the cross street up at the four-way stop. Julie watched the woman open the rear door of the cab and jump inside. Then she turned over the key, set her own car to purring and eased out of the parking spot to tail the cab and the woman inside.

Julie had experience, and training, in following suspect vehicles, and she used it now, keeping her distance but keeping the taxicab in sight. The traffic was light at that late hour on a weekday. Until they crossed Main Street and headed down to the docks. Then there was no traffic at all. Julie had to douse her lights, knowing it was illegal and not caring. She was as curious as Vincent now about what was going on.

The cab turned right at the river and travelled along Front Street, past the docks, the warehouse district, to the barren, desolate waterfront well up the river. Julie saw it swerve left, bump along a short dirt road, then come to a stop. The taxicab's headlights illuminated an isolated, dilapidated shack perched on the edge of the weed-strewn riverbank, and Julie frowned in concern.

The woman got out of the cab, ran to the door of the shack, pulled it open and slipped inside. Light glowed in the one window on the side of the shack, as the cab pulled out and drove back up Front Street. Past Julie in her darkened car.

She drove down the street and turned into the dirt road and parked. She opened the car door and got out, softly closed the door and jammed her gun into the waistband of her jeans at the back. Her sneakers made no noise as she crept along the rutted path up to the shack. She didn't like the set-up at all. Liked it even less when she heard a loud crack, then a scream.

The shrill cry came from a woman. The violent crack sounded like flesh impacting flesh. Julie leaped forward and pressed herself up against the weathered plank wall of the shack, next to the grimy window. There was another crack, another scream. Julie ducked down under the window, then rose. She peered through the cracked glass, and her eyes widened with shock.

Cassie was pushed up against the far wall of the shack, naked except for her high heels and stockings, her hands splayed out on the wall, body arched at the waist, bum thrust back. A large, powerfully built man dressed entirely in black leather had hold of her golden-blonde hair with one hand and was smacking Cassie's round, ripe bottom with his other huge hand. He cracked his hardened palm across her outthrust rump, making her scream, jump. Rhythmically, brutally, over and over, hand marks flashing white on the rippling, reddened flesh of Cassie's vulnerable bum.

Julie raced around to the front of the shack and kicked the door open, barked, 'Freeze, asshole!' Her gun up and levelled at the giant.

He twisted his bald head around and glared at her. Cassie jerked her head around and stared at Julie.

There was shock in Cassie's glazed, amber eyes, contempt in the man's steel-grey ones. A sneer curled his full, red lips, the gold earring in his left ear glinting in the light shed by the one overhead bulb hanging from the tarpaper ceiling. He raised his right hand up into the air again, looked at it, at Julie's raised weapon. He slammed his hand down across Cassie's singed buttocks, shivering her ass, shaking the woman and the wall she was clinging to.

Julie's finger tightened on the trigger.

Cassie screamed, 'No, Julie! I want it! I want Tony to spank me!'

Julie gulped, the gun shaking in front of her. Her eyes focused on Cassie's blushing rump, the full buttocks glowing with heat, and she noticed the streaks of wetness on Cassie's inner thighs, running down the woman's trembling legs.

'Yeah, she fucking wants it – bad!' Tony growled. He jerked Cassie's head back, crashed his hand down against her butt cheeks, rocking her hard. 'Bad enough to pay for it.'

Julie looked at the scowling man. Her eyes travelled down his broad shoulders and barrel chest and flat stomach, to the bulge in the front of the man's leather pants – a large bulge that seemed to throb and grow right before Julie's eyes, threatening to split the man's pants wide open. She slowly lowered her gun, tucked it back into the waistband of her jeans on the third attempt. 'Wh–what's going on?' Her voice was dry and cracked.

Tony grinned with even white teeth. He lifted his sledge of a hand up high, Julie and Cassie's eyes following it, then brought it whistling down onto Cassie's butt. Only the hand gripping her hair kept the woman from flying right through the rickety wall of the shack and out into the turgid river below.

Julie walked closer. Cassie tore a hand off the wall and gestured urgently at her, grabbed onto Julie's T-shirt. 'I–I can't get this at home!' she hissed in Julie's face. 'Vincent could never do it, wouldn't hear of it, you know that. But I need it, I want it. It's not –'

She choked on her words, as Tony whacked her ass with another vicious blow, and another, and another. Her eyes rolled back in her head, her lips quivering. 'It's not ... cheating, Julie!' she moaned. 'Tony means nothing to me.' A particularly savage strike sent Cassie grabbing onto Julie with both hands.

Julie grasped Cassie's bare, rounded shoulders, glaring at the big man laying down wicked blow after blow onto Cassie's unprotected rear-end. The blistering smack of hard flesh on soft flesh echoed violently in the bare-board confines of the stuffy shack, like gunshots. Cassie jerked up on her high heels with every swat, her body shaking, large breasts jumping. Her fingernails bit into Julie's arms, desperately clinging to the woman, her mouth hanging open, eyelids fluttering, as Tony tore up her backside with professional fervour.

'Oh, God, Julie! It feels so good! So bad! I have to have it, and I can't get it at home!'

Julie's hands went damp on Cassie's smooth skin. She felt each jolt of the woman's lush body as the blows landed with stunning force, could feel the raw heat of Cassie's searing need so close. She tore her eyes off Cassie's contorted face and stared at that tremendous bulge in Tony's pants, at the white streaking lightning of his hand as it stormed pain and pleasure across Cassie's rump, thundering on impact, electrifying the groaning woman.

It was wildly perverse. Julie's face and body burned with the reflected heat, with the shocks that shook Cassie's body in her clutching hands. Her pussy tingled with wetness.

'Tell him to spank me with the switch, Julie! Whip me with the switch! I'm so very bad, Julie, I know it!'

'Th–the switch?' Julie croaked.

And there it was, in Tony's right hand, the hand he'd used to punish Cassie's bum so severely already. It was four feet long, flat and narrow, made of tautly flexible wood. Tony flicked his wrist and the switch quivered, rapidly. Julie watched in awe as the man brought the vibrating instrument up from his side and over his head. She felt Cassie's body flinch with anticipation, the woman gritting her teeth, her eyes squeezed tight shut. The switch singing up in the electrified air.

Tony lashed Cassie's ass.

The woman just about jumped right out of Julie's hands. Her mouth stretched wide in a silent scream, her eyes bulging, neck veins corded, breasts heaving. Butt cheeks gyrating uncontrollably. Julie could do nothing to comfort her, only hold on tight, as Tony struck her over and over, the snapping whip of the switch filling Julie's burning ears almost to the point of her screaming.

'Does your friend want a taste?'

Julie and Cassie pulled their eyes away from each other, swung them around onto Tony. He was leering at Julie, the flesh-heated switch quivering alongside his leg again, Cassie's ravaged ass and body quivering in rhythm.

'You won't regret it,' Cassie rasped, pulling her fingers out of Julie's arms and plastering them back up against the wall.

Julie let go of Cassie's shoulders, stumbled backwards. She gasped when she saw the network of criss-crossed red welts on Cassie's blistered bottom, the visible hand-prints on the brutalised skin. Cassie's shaking buttocks were swollen, savaged.

'Feel the tough love,' Tony snarled.

Julie reached out a trembling hand and touched a flaming ridge on Cassie's ass, ran her fingers along the raised, flayed flesh. Cassie jerked and shrieked, the tenderness after all the torture, the tension, turning her body and brain into a live wire through which sensation rippled and coursed, heightened to the sexual breaking point.

Julie had never seen, felt anything like it, and she'd been around. The wicked sensuality of it all pulsed through Cassie's body and into Julie's fingers, all through her own body. Her pussy shimmered. She couldn't let the opportunity pass.

She pulled her T-shirt loose from her jeans and up over her head. Her breasts jutted out from her chest taut and rounded, creamy-white, pink nipples seized up tight, pointing. And as she unbuttoned and unzipped her jeans, slid them down her long legs, she watched Tony unzip the steel fly on his leather trousers, pull his hard cock out into the open. The man had a club, swollen hood and shaft as smooth as his head. Julie's panties were glued to her pussy with moisture, and she had to peel them away.

'Two for one. Ladies night,' Tony jeered, his cock jutting out from the opening in his trousers.

Julie positioned herself next to Cassie, spreading her hands out on the wood, walking her feet back, arching her body, pushing her tight, twin-mounded bum out at the cock-heavy, switch-wielding giant. Cassie tried to smile reassuringly, but her lips were writhing too much. She pressed her right hand on top of Julie's left hand. Tony slashed the switch across Julie's bare virgin buttocks.

'Ohmigod!' Julie cried, shocked to the core. Pain arced through her body, up from the sizzling stripe Tony had carved into her bottom.

He lashed her again, then Cassie. His erection bobbed, twitched, as he waled the two women's asses. They clung to the wall, to each other, the blows exploding on their buttocks and burning through their bodies, spiking their pussies, again and again. To the point where Julie was craving it like Cassie was, the excruciating part the strokes in between, when Tony was flailing Cassie's rump instead of hers. When the switch finally struck her again, she almost sighed with relief, the pleasure and pain flooding her, filling her pussy to brimming.

Tony scarred the women's asses for what seemed like for ever. His bald head shone with perspiration, breath hissing out of his mouth like the switch through the air. The women's shrieks and wails sounded over his rasping, along with the cracking of flesh, the song of the whip.

Finally, the big man dropped the switch. But he was far from done. He picked up a leather strap – a blunt instrument to sear the pain he'd inflicted deep into the two women's bodies and beings. The strap was a foot and a half long and two inches wide, half an inch thick. It was the kind of hardened, pebbled leather that school principals used to wield against insolent children, only industrial strength.

Tony bashed Cassie's battered cheeks with the brutal tool first, laying it hard across her buttocks, making her squeal and jump, the juices run in a river down her quaking legs. And then he crushed Julie's buttocks flat with a swing of the strap, sending her shouting up onto her toes, making her squirt.

The women stared at one another, holding hands with whitened knuckles. They were joined in the fiery inferno, sisters of spankage surreal. Their palms bled sweat and their nails bit blood, as the strap thudded against their bums, rocking them over and over, rocketing cruel joy into their souls.

Tony's cock speared almost straight up into the air, a glistening tear of pre-come adorning his gaping slit. He alternated his ass assault, smashing one woman's bottom, then the other, then two blows in a row to the one boiled bum. Keeping the women on their toes without respite, clenching with the prospect of another blow blasting their ass.

He slammed Cassie's butt with the blunt instrument, then Julie's, then at last dropped the strap. He laid his big, dampened hands on the women's asses, and the wanton tremoring of their butt flesh made his paws dance, the white heat singeing his thick fingers. 'Time to plug up the pain,' he ground out, digging his fingernails into the raw, ravaged skin.

Julie whipped her head around. Tony was greasing his cock with lube. The huge organ glistened, even more dangerous than any of the other tools he applied so far. 'No! I don't –'

'It feels so good after getting spanked, Julie,' Cassie cooed. 'A hard cock shoved up your butt, thrust back and forth. Sensational!'

The woman was almost delirious. Julie's bottom was numb, but not the rest of her senses. She'd never been fucked in the bum before, and was afraid she couldn't take it. Especially after already getting flogged. Especially because Tony's prick was so big.

But then, she'd never been viciously spanked before. And she'd taken that, and enjoyed it immensely after taking the plunge. Cassie squeezed her hand, the woman blinking tears out of her eyes. 'Fuck my ass!' Julie growled at Tony.

The big man grinned. His leather creaked as he got up close. He smacked Julie's left buttock, then pulled it aside, exposing the woman's pink puckered bumhole.

Tony thrust his bloated hood up against Julie's starfish, shoved it through.

'Oh! God!' Julie screamed. The man's hammerhead filled her ass ring, stretching it, sticking her full of new and strange sensations.

Tony rotated his cockhead around inside Julie's anus, loosening her up, at the same time tightening her body like a bow. He slammed forward, plunging his shaft halfway into her. She spasmed, the enormity of the man's cock bloating her bum. Tony sank the rest of his dong into her, right to the balls, and she thought she'd faint, the stuffed-full feeling that flooded her body and brain so weird, yet so wonderful.

'You love it, Julie! You love it!' Cassie wailed. 'I told you! All that cock in your burning bright ass!'

Julie gaped at the woman, man-filled like she'd never been filled before. It was obvious Cassie frantically craved what she was getting. But Tony held deep and thick and pulsating in Julie's butt, his balls and body pressing up against her flinching cheeks.

Then, suddenly, he pulled back, out, leaving Julie gasping with a gaping emptiness. She watched Cassie's eyes slowly close, the woman's mouth slowly open, as Tony plunged the depths of her depravity with his tremendous member. Julie could taste the exquisite pleasure on Cassie's lips, knowing exactly now what she'd been talking about – how it felt having a man's sledge of a cock stuck up your spanked ass. She kissed Cassie, the two women sharing a sinful intimacy reserved only for the most daring.

Tony grabbed onto Cassie's butt cheeks and dug his fingers in deep, drilled into her ass even deeper. He rocked back and forth, his gleaming cock gliding in and out of the woman's obscenely stretched chute. She contracted her butt muscles, sucking on his plugging pipe.

Then he was out, leaving Cassie's flowered pink rosebud to slowly close. He shifted over to Julie again, grabbed on, pushed in, pounded back and forth. Julie's short brown hair flew in rhythm to the anal onslaught, her body jerking, as Tony pumped harder, faster, splitting her cheeks with a savage intensity. She thought he would tear her apart, thundering into her anus, stretching and straining the realms of sexual possibilities like they'd never been stretched and strained for her before. She bit into her lip as the man smashed his thighs against her butt, hammering his cock home.

Julie almost collapsed to her knees when Tony pulled his dong free from her rectum and ploughed it into Cassie, pistoned her ass. 'Rub your pussy!' Cassie hissed at Julie. 'Rub your pussy while he's fucking your bum!'

Julie watched as Cassie tore her left hand off the slatted wall and plunged it down in between her quivering legs. Cassie instantly shuddered and screamed at just one touch of her button, astonishing Julie. The woman was coming right before Julie's eyes, squirting ecstasy out of her pussy as she swallowed cock up her ass.

Julie stared at Tony, her eyes wide. The man was out of Cassie's anus, moving over to her again with his menacing prong. Cassie was a mess, shuddering out of control, tears rolling down her face, tits jouncing. She clutched her cunt, juices shooting out between her fingers, riding wild orgasm in the extreme.

Tony jammed his cock into Julie's ass and clamped down on her cheeks. He pummelled her butt with his thrusting body, stoking fire in her anus with his cock. Julie reached down in between her legs and touched her clit. The pink button was swollen larger and harder than it'd ever been, but seemed to be numb. Julie grinned and began to rub.

And then something exploded inside her. She screamed, all the lean muscles on her long body involuntarily clenching to the snapping point, orgasm bursting through her like an electric charge, pulsating powerfully to the frenetic pace of Tony's pumping cock in her ass. The intensity was insane, torching her. And it went on and on, driving her out of her mind.

When she finally came back to reality, she was clinging to Cassie for dear life, the liquid fire of Tony's own brutal orgasm dripping out of both of the women's bruised and blasted asses.

* * *

'It's like this, Vincent.' Julie gestured at Cassie to turn around. Then she lifted the woman's dress at the back, revealing the raw evidence of what Vincent's wife had been up to.

The man's jaw dropped, his eyes bulging behind his lenses. He gaped at his wife's ridged, striped, reddened bum.

'She needs a good spanking every now and then,' Julie informed her friend, lowering the curtain on Tony's handiwork. 'You have to spice things up, or any marriage will go stale, and spouses will look elsewhere … for excitement.'

Cassie turned back around and looked at her husband. He slapped her face.

'That's a start,' Julie said, walking stiffly towards the door. 'I'll leave you two to "work" things out.' She wanted to get back to her car, sit down on the cushioned bucket seat and luxuriate in the simmering sensations still brimming in her badly beaten bum.

Pretty Tied-Up
Valerie Grey

My boyfriend at the time was Mike and it was my first real kinky relationship. You know how that is. Your first of anything out there is quite an experience, and this was no exception.

He was older than me. I was twenty and he was 46, had already been married twice. He was a professor at the college and I was a student. He introduced me to bondage and flashing. He would often spring the unexpected on me, and it was wonderful. Mike thought it would be interesting to expose me to some things all at once and some things a little at a time.

After breakfast one morning, he told me were going to play a kinky little game.

A statement like that tends to get your attention.

Right there in the kitchen, he helped me strip naked and then led me into the bedroom. He had me lie on my back on the bed, and then produced some soft nylon rope, fixed to the four corners of the bed. My mind was quickly getting foggy and, before I really knew what was happening, he had me tied up. All I could do was squirm, not knowing what was to happen next. It was such a sexy feeling to be naked and tied and feeling helpless. This got me wet, and we hadn't even done anything yet.

What did Mike have in mind? He told me a day crew of men were coming to install new windows in the living room. I still didn't quite understand his intentions, until he started raising all of the bedroom window blinds and opened the bedroom door wide. He stood there in the doorway and looked around the room. I must have had fear on my face, because he smiled. He went to the dresser and took out one of my bras. He walked back over to the door and smiled at me again as he dropped the bra in the doorway.

The bedroom was just off the living room, and the doorway was not far at all from the front door. He knew there was no way the men would not see the bra lying there. That smile on his face was a mean one, but it was so sexy.

Then the doorbell rang, and his face lit up. 'I have to let the men in, and then go to work. I will be back for lunch. The fun is about to begin, sweetie. Enjoy your morning.' He vanished, not allowing me to say a thing.

There I was: all alone, naked and tied spread-eagled to the bed, my pussy open and dripping wet. It was a bright sunny morning. I thought of calling out to Mike. I could hear him talking to some strange men in the living room. Then I heard the front door slam and, shortly after that, his car driving away. Until that moment, I didn't really take him seriously. Until then, I thought he surely would come back into the bedroom, shut the door and fuck me.

A few minutes went by, and I heard the strange men just feet away in the living room, working and talking. I squirmed helplessly on that bed. What if one of them came looking for the bathroom, or noticed the bra Mike had so conveniently left?

Maybe that was Mike's plan.

The thoughts I had were indescribable, full scenarios and possibilities. I was scared and nervous. I was wet and horny. I wanted cock – one cock, Mike's cock, or twenty cocks, those men's dicks, I wanted them in me now. If these men wanted to take me, I wouldn't be able to stop them.

Every window-shade in the room was wide open and I could see the men walking past. Their truck was parked in the drive and when they needed tools they had to walk past the bedroom. I lay there watching as each sweaty body walked by, just waiting for one of them to glance in the window and spot me.

I spent three hours like that. There were seven or more

strange men just feet away from me, while I was bound and helpless. It was amazing. My nipples were hard and aching, and my mouth was dry, unlike my pussy, which remained moist from thinking about what could happen, such as: what would I do if one of them came in and laid his hot sweaty body on mine? Or if he put his head between my spread legs and lapped at my cunt like a mangy dog?

I would actually beg them to take me, if I had to. All morning, I was secretly hoping they'd see me and wouldn't be able to control their dark desires to ravish me. I even thought of the possibility of more men being there than I could see – twenty, thirty. I imagined being gang-fucked by fifty sweaty, vulgar men. I was even thinking of calling out or making some noise to get one of them to notice me there.

I heard a car turn into the drive. It was Mike. He had planned it perfectly. The men were just finishing up with the windows and he waited until they were gone to come into the bedroom.

He didn't say a thing; he looked at me and the lust I had on my face and he got on top of me and took me like a piece of meat. I wanted to grab him and hold on, but he didn't untie me. He just fucked me, very hard. I nearly passed out. My climax was overwhelming.

I was still tied, and there was a wet spot between my legs and his semen oozed out slowly. He asked me how I liked my first experience at this. I was speechless.

After that day, we got on the Internet and started looking for like-minded couples and what kind of fun this might bring.

* * *

We met Alex and Lisa. First we met at dinner a few times, and got to know one another. She was 40 and he was 32. Then we started switching partners during these dinners so I was feeling up Alex, and Mike was rubbing Lisa's leg. We quickly moved up to actual date swapping. Alex and I saw one movie, and Mike and Lisa saw a different one.

Being the flirtatious type, I was kissing, touching and driving Alex crazy. He obviously wanted me. I teased him even more by telling him he could eventually tie me up and have his way with me. That night, when I confessed this to Mike, he got very horny. He said he would try to make it happen some day soon.

We continued our fun with Alex and Lisa, and one night I agreed to cook them dinner. A couple of grad students from the university, John and Mandy, were also there. The dinner and evening went great. Everyone seemed to love my cooking. After dinner, we relaxed in the living room. Mike mixed a pitcher of vodka and juice, and I made some snacks. A porno movie was put in the DVD, and everyone was watching and getting horny.

Strangely enough, the movie was about a girl who got stripped and tied spread-eagled to a bed, where various men and women urinated on her. It was German. We were all getting drunk and watching it with interest.

Mike moved close to me and whispered in my ear. He wanted to know if I would like another session being tied to the bed. He said I could tell the others I was getting tired and head off to bed. He would come in and tie me down, and then go back and continue to party with the others. After everybody went home, he would come in and ravage me.

Of course, I nodded.

* * *

In the bedroom, Mike slowly took off my clothes. He threw me on the bed and tied me down. My nipples were hard, and I was wet before he was even finished.

I squirmed, testing my bonds. I was completely helpless and horny, with friends in the next room; I could hear them talking about the bondage and pissing movie. Lisa and Mandy were giggling.

I didn't notice that Mike had left the room. The door was wide open, just as it had been when the window installers were working. If anyone on their way to the bathroom looked in, they would see me.

For the next hour or so, the party continued. I could

hear our guests talking and laughing, but I couldn't make out what they were saying. I could make out Mike's laugh and my pussy ached when I heard him. I imagined him standing by the bed and laughing: a knowing chortle, telling me I was *his*for whatever dirty thing he wanted.

Then everybody got very quiet. All I could hear was the porn movie.

Mike came into the bedroom and shut the door behind him. He turned on the lights and watched me, just as I had imagined he would. He told me he had a surprise; he said the party was moving into the bedroom.

There was a knock at the door. In walked our guests with expressions like kids at an amusement park. They stood around the bed, glancing at my bound and squirming body. I looked to Mike for an answer and he told me to relax. He said this was the next step in my experience.

He offered to refill everyone's drink and promptly left the room.

Then I was blindfolded. This was an added sensation. The men then encouraged the women to have some fun with me. I could feel soft bodies exploring mine. It didn't take long for me to start enjoying it. I couldn't tell who was who.

During this exploration, I heard clothing drawers opened. Alex and John were making lewd remarks about my sexy underthings, commenting that I probably liked anal sex. They seemed to be impressed with what they found, suggesting their partners should have some items like mine.

The evening continued, with the men joining in on the fun. I was fucked several times, my face splattered with sperm more than once, and one of them urinated in my mouth, emulating the German porno. I couldn't count the times I came, but each one was very powerful. I was in a sexual dream state for a couple of hours. I couldn't do anything but accept what these nameless bodies were forcing upon me, body fluids covering me, filling my mouth.

I drank.

When I came back to reality, I was untied, the blindfold removed. In the mirror I could see I was covered with sweat and come and piss. I felt like a total dirty fucking slut.

I wanted more.

Mike told me it was a very eventful evening, and I had been the perfect sexual toy. He asked if I enjoyed my experience and all I could do was smile. I was still euphoric. My mind was still sorting the feelings.

I was able to sit up and look around the room. A lot of my bras and panties were strewn around, some lying on the floor or on and about the bed, and stockings were draped over the dresser and mirror. It looked like a sexual Tasmanian Devil had come through, or the Cat in the Hat on Ecstasy.

I found some items were missing. That made me feel humiliated. I envisioned Lisa and Mandy enjoying my panties. I had visions of both women turning their men on while wearing my junk. Maybe they even pretended to be me.

* * *

A month later, Mike said he had a surprise for me. He took me into the bedroom, where he had two spreader bars and some large pillows on the floor. He told me this was another way to tie someone, making it more fun.

Well, of course, I was game, and was soon naked and secured. My wrists were bound to one bar, my ankles to the other. I couldn't move and Mike picked me up and plopped me on the bed. He had me lie on my back and he fixed each bar to some fancy connectors he had hidden under the bed. He adjusted the bars so my arms and legs were spread wide and I could struggle only slightly.

Straining, I could see Mike walking around the room, as if he was setting something up. I could also see a leather bag on the dresser; it had not been there before.

The doorbell rang. He said our party guests had arrived and left me alone.

I could hear the voices of several people. They came into the bedroom. Our four guests from last month were all standing around the bed, soon joined by what seemed like three other couples, men and women of various ages whom I didn't know.

It looked like *I* was going to be the party again. I couldn't help but smile. The women started taking their clothes off. Down came jeans and off came blouses and bras and panties. I couldn't believe what I saw: Lisa was wearing *my* pink bra and panty set, while a woman I didn't know was wearing my black teddy. They both looked great in them, though. I didn't get to see much more before Mike blindfolded me.

I felt the bed moving, as at least one person was getting on top of me. Before I knew what was happening, I had someone's wet pussy mashing against my face. And, at about the same time, a hot tongue was licking at my clit. My own tongue was soon very busy, too. Whoever she was, she tasted wonderful. That tongue down there, man or woman, knew just where to go and what to do. The woman's hips clamped down on my head, so I couldn't move, even if I had wanted to. She rubbed her wet bush all over my face, then she began to pee.

As quickly as she got on top of me, she got off. She was replaced by the other girl, who got into almost the same position and did the same thing ... but, instead of smashing her pussy against my face, it seemed she was wearing some sort of strap-on. She told me to open wide, and soon my mouth was full of a large thrusting cock.

It wasn't a real cock, but it sure felt the same, just

without the pulsing heat of flesh. This cock was fucking my mouth and I had to open wide to take it all. A tongue was working on my clit and I couldn't control myself. My body wriggled and shook as the tongue kept sinking into my pussy. I struggled to swallow the strap-on, overwhelmed by the sensations of being at the mercy of these people. The men were the cheering section, giving the girls ideas: do this, do that to the slut. They called me a dirty filthy fucking slut and it was true. It turned me on to be that: not a person with a name or life or dreams, but simply a slut whose only reason for existence was to be used sexually.

The strap-on was removed from my mouth and the woman on top of me seemed to be switching her position. She got down between my bound legs and wrapped her arms around them. Pulling my body up to her, she plunged her tongue deep into my pussy.

I pleaded with her not to stop. And she didn't. I could feel her teeth against my pubic area, as her tongue skilfully wiggled inside me. I tried to thrust up to get even more of that hot tongue inside me, but I couldn't move. Her hold on my legs was strong, and she took her time snaking that tongue into my pussy. She sucked hard on my sensitive clit. Her arms had a vice-like hold on my legs, she moved with me and my body reacted to what her mouth was doing. I came against her face.

The spreader bar holding my legs was disconnected

from the bed and my legs were raised up over my body; the bar was secured at the head of the bed. This made me nearly fold in half, and my naked ass was waving up in the air. In another quick movement, a mouth was again between my legs. I felt soft feminine arms grab my waist and a tender but forceful mouth go to work on my still throbbing sex. In this position, my ass began a sensuous shaking, with the skilled female form along for the ride. Our combined weight made the bed bounce wildly.

Just as I was getting close to climax again, I was left alone, my twitching crotch waiting for what was to happen next.

My ass was next. Something cold was globbed on my asshole and soon after that my anus was impaled by something long and hard and big, too big. I could only assume it was the strap-on that was previously in my mouth. But it seemed so much thicker; my mouth would never have been able to open wide enough to take it but my asshole stretched, somewhat painfully at first, to accommodate the thing.

I could feel someone's nipples brush past my leg as my ass was being fucked. Sweet, sexy kisses planted on my calves, driving me further into her power. Her body between my legs, her arms moved to either side of my head. In this position, she repeatedly pushed into my shithole. I could smell the perfume of my mistress mixed with the ass smell from my rear end.

Deeper and deeper, that fake cock rammed into my asspipe. It was strange to know it was attached to a woman. Strange, but nice. I had never had a woman sodomise me with a strap-on, or any woman do anything with a strap-on, or any strap-on at all, so this was all new. I could tell she liked it too and maybe this was her first time as well. Her breath was quick and little drops of sweet-smelling sweat were dripping onto my body. She was a determined mistress. Determined to have her way with me, no matter how messy I made her fake cock with my ass juice.

I wanted a tongue on my clit but I wasn't the one in control. That woman-controlled cock was in control. I was beginning to want it deeper inside me, mostly because I knew it was a woman doing it. I didn't know how much I would like that combination.

I am being ass-fucked by a woman, I thought.

I had never had anal sex with anyone but Mike. He had shown me the way. He fucked my ass all the time, and now a woman was having it.

A soft body, but a powerful one too. A female in control of what I experienced. Well, actually, there were two women in control of my mind and body. I could feel their lips on my pussy, knowing where to go and what to do. They were controlling my orgasm and forcing it to build until I would come over those lips, those soft female lips.

I had never really thought of being with another woman. I had no idea of how it would be; there had been some experiences when I was eighteen but they were innocent, nothing, just play, never a fuck, never an orgasm. Attached to a woman, this cock-shaped rubber thing was finding a spot deep inside me, and that spot definitely liked it, the way kittens enjoy catnip.

I wanted to be released from my bonds so I could wrap my arms and legs around her body. I wanted to feel the power of her thrusts, and to let her know I wanted more. There were many strange and different feelings rushing through my mind.

My mistress of cock was now breathing harder, and she seemed to be close to orgasm. My pussy was dripping, my ass was full, and I couldn't get enough of it. She started shaking and then so did I. We both came together, and she rammed that cock hard into my asshole. She leaned down and kissed me on my nose, my cheeks and then my lips. Her tongue only slightly entered my mouth, and then it was gone. She was teasing me.

She lifted herself off my body and gave my ass a slap. I tried to think who it could have been, but I didn't have much time; there was another soft female body on the bed, with more interesting things to come. This new mistress was completely different. Her fingers found my clit and started to rub in circles. With my body in such a position, I was open to anything she wanted. I know she could tell I liked what she was doing. I couldn't conceal that.

Her lips joined in, and my hips began moving with her fingers. She made her tongue hard and jabbed it into my wet pussy while pinching my clit. What a change that was. And it was so unexpected. And, as quickly as it started, it went back to just her finger rubbing on my clit.

She was playing me. I tried to compose myself, waiting for what would happen next. I didn't have to wait long. That finger on my clit quickly slid into my pussy and she jabbed it in and out, like a little cock. While doing this, she started spanking me. These weren't light spanks but hard, punishing*smacks*. At first it startled me, but soon I was getting into it.

I heard whispering, then those fingers I loved so much returned. Deeper and deeper they fucked my pussy and, when they were deep inside me, her thumb roughly rubbed my clit. It seemed like she knew exactly what to do. The whole evening had been that way.

The spanking started again. It wasn't with a hand, but a paddle. It hurt but, because I had been previously spanked by hand, it wasn't too much. I began to wiggle against her hand, twisting and jerking, wanting it deeper and harder.

Then, again, it all stopped.

I yelled, 'Don't stop, you fucking bitches! Make me come!'

My leg bar was unhooked from the head of the bed, and for a short time I was allowed to relax. Then I was flipped over. I was a human pancake. I landed back on the bed. There was now a large pillow under me, and my ass was up high in the air. The bar holding my legs was secured to the bottom of the bed, and I was again unable to accomplish more than a slight wiggle. Now I was securely tied, and my ass was a perfect target.

Someone got on the bed again, in front of me. Between my tightly stretched arms, right in front of my head. I could smell the masculine scent of this person, and the cock now poking my face wasn't a strap-on. This one was the real deal. It had a smooth velvet texture, throbbing hot against my cheek.

I opened my mouth, offering my throat to its advances. It accepted my invitation and slid past my lips. I gave only a little resistance. I wanted to feel it as it went all the way down.

Strong hands grabbed the sides of my head and soon this manly cock owned my mouth. Thrust after thrust, I gulped it down, wrapping my tongue around it when I could.

There was another person getting on the bed. This person got behind me, between my spread legs. I felt fingers exploring my pussy; they found my clit. It was extra sensitive and I wiggled in reaction to the touch. My response elicited giggles from the group – a lot of them.

Just how many were watching, how many preparing to take me?

The fingers left me and came back with my vibrator. I hadn't realised Mike would tell them where it was. My vibrator is like a big hard cock. It is flesh-coloured, and even has veins and a bulging head. With two speeds, it is a wonderful toy for singular enjoyment. I hadn't ever thought of it for more than that.

The vibrator was finding all of my special spots; different and interesting sensations, for sure. I couldn't wait for what would be next. It was turned to high speed, and I nearly jumped out of my bonds. I thought it was already on high. My eyes fluttered as the cock in my mouth kept going.

The person behind me held the vibrator on my clit, and raked fingernails across my sore ass. I then knew it was a female. She plunged her fingers inside my pussy, but quickly pulled them out. She slapped my ass, *hard*.

She raked her fingernails across my ass again.

She plunged her fingers into my pussy again.

She dropped the vibrator and slapped my ass hard with her other hand as she kept finger-fucking my cunt.

She started wiggling her fingers inside me. She picked up the vibrator and it was still humming. She slid it along the inside of my left leg up to my twat. She rubbed it down my right leg to my knee. She took it back the other way. Each time, it buzzed on my clit for just a second.

I could feel it on my leg, and knew when it was going to be touching my clit. She removed her fingers again. I could still hear the vibrator, but I couldn't feel it. She seemed to be moving around, changing position. Before I knew what was happening, she was lying down under me, right behind the pillow holding me up. She wrapped her arms around my waist and pulled us together. Her mouth came in contact with my clit and the electricity began. I started humping her mouth and my mouth was getting humped, too. She was doing great at keeping that tongue of hers busy on my clit, and then she slid it into my pussy.

I started choking on the cock in my mouth. I guess that was sexy to the man there because soon after that he came. He moaned aloud and I could tell it was Alex. For some reason, it turned me on knowing my mouth was full of Alex's cock, his semen flowing down my throat and into my stomach. My body went out of control and I came all over the face of whoever was licking my clit.

Two got up off the bed, and two more replaced them.

I still didn't know who each woman was, but I figured John was now in front of me. He mashed his stomach up against my face, and I licked circles in the curly hair. He reached down and pinched my nipples, one at a time. But that wasn't enough. They ached so, and I would have loved someone to nibble on them. I asked John if he would suck on my tits and his answer was to bounce his hard cock against my face. He nearly flogged me with it, whipping it back and forth as it smacked my cheeks. I opened my mouth and he shoved it in. Another cock to suck. John was smaller and thicker than Alex was; easier to swallow, but harder to keep my mouth open enough.

Somebody got behind me and I felt a cock against my ass. He reached down and fingered my clit, where my juices were flowing freely. He grabbed my hips and I felt the head of his cock rubbing my pussy lips.

He took me.

He leaned forward and bit my shoulder, then licked my neck.

'How do you like your party, slut?'

That was Mike's voice. Mike was behind me. He reached around the pillow and grabbed my tits. That hit home. I sucked on John's cock like it was a chocolate sucker, and Mike fucked my pussy like the pro he was; his body slapped against my ass, he was fucking me so hard. My bound legs didn't allow me too much room to move, so my body took the brunt of his thrusts.

The hotter I got, the more I sucked on that cock. And it seemed the more I sucked on it, the deeper he tried to ram it into me. Because my hands were bound, I couldn't back away from this ramming.

I was getting it from both ends. Mike upped the stakes. He slipped out of my pussy and quickly shoved his cock up my burning ass. He didn't even break stride. He had no resistance from my ass: the strap-on fucking had stretched it wide, making me gape.

My body tensed and then a rush of spasms seemed to engulf all of my senses. I couldn't help it. It was just too much. I lost all control and nearly passed out. I think I was in another space for a while. I had no form, I was just pure orgasm, and I was one with a universe made of pleasure and joy.

John pulled his cock out and stroked it until he came all over my face. He was holding my head by my hair with one hand, and aiming his spurting cock at my face with the other. I remember Mike's hands were exploring all over my body as he continued to ram my asshole. I have very sensitive tits and the way he grabbed them made me explode again. I was so involved in my own orgasm, I don't remember if he came or not. I am sure he did, but that was just how powerful mine was.

* * *

Hours later, I was in such a state of orgasmic frenzy that, long after the party guests had left, I had no idea who I was or what my name was.

Mike held me until I returned to the human, my body now aching from having been used so much.

'What do you think?' Mike asked me.

'I don't want to think,' I replied, 'I only want to feel, to experience.'

He smiled and kissed me and said, 'Now you are beginning to learn and understand, my lovely slut.'

Indeed.

Wild Ride
Kathleen Tudor

The parking lot of the prison looked like a step into hell, and I sighed as I parked the car. It was a hot day and the sun beat down hard on the open expanse of concrete and the drab, dirty building. I got out of my car and checked my watch. I was only a few minutes early, but I had no idea if the wheels of justice turned on time or if I would be in for a painful wait.

I was just beginning to think I should have brought a magazine or something when I heard a gate rattle open across the lot. Two guards escorted Angelo Ramirez to the gate and stopped short, allowing him to walk away from the prison. My stupid heart sped up as he stepped into view, and my equally uninformed stomach did a little flip. 'I can't believe this shit,' I muttered. It had been four years since I'd seen the bastard, and I still couldn't take my eyes off of him.

He stopped a few feet past the gate and glanced around the parking lot. There were very few cars to consider, but when he reached me he only raked his eyes up and down my figure approvingly before continuing to scan his surroundings. 'Yo, Angelo,' I called, drawing his eyes back to me. 'You want a ride, or what?'

'My man Johnny's supposed to be picking me up. Who the fuck are you?' He approached as he spoke, disrespectful and pigheaded as usual. My stomach quivered and I wished I could pinch myself.

'Your man Johnny wouldn't like the attitude you're taking with his little sister,' I said. His eyebrows shot up and he gave me the once-over again, slower this time. I had only been seventeen when he'd last seen me, gangly and a slow bloomer. I'd blossomed while he'd been away, though, and my gangliness had turned into legginess as my hips and breasts rounded out. I was wearing a tight top and curve-hugging jeans to show them off, and was torn between pride and hating myself as his face registered obvious approval at the changes.

'You grew up,' he said.

'You're a pig. You want a ride, or you wanna go back inside?'

He laughed at me as he swung into the car and pulled the door shut behind him. 'It's hot out, babe. How about getting that AC cranked?'

I shook my head as I followed his lead, dropping into

my little car and starting the engine. 'I'm supposed to take you to check in at the halfway house. I'm sure Mrs Adams will be so happy to see you again.'

'Oh, I'm sure. It'll be just like old times, eh?' He slouched in the passenger seat, refusing to fasten his seatbelt, and I knew better than to tell him to – he'd just get pissed and even more stubborn. Angelo was the type who was convinced that he was destined to die young, so what was the point in worrying? 'Wait up for me, will you? I'll check in with her and then you can bring me around to meet Johnny.'

'He's changed, Angelo, I'm warning you. Johnny's gone straight. He's got a good job doing landscaping, and he isn't going to let you drag him back into your shit again.'

'What, dealing? Come on, mama, what's the harm in it? People are gonna buy anyway, why not get a cut of what's going around?' He grinned over at me, and I firmly ignored the below-the-belt tingle that followed his flirtatious glances.

'Four years?' I said sarcastically, but as usual Angelo only laughed it off.

'Yeah, well, the food was shit, I'll tell you that.' He'd been in and out of prison since I'd known him, and it didn't seem to bother him any whether he was in or out. 'Landscaping, huh?' He gave a dismissive snort. 'Break your back so them rich bastards don't have to pull their own weeds or mow their own lawns. Now *that* is some bullshit.'

'He's taking care of his family, you dumb shit,' I said, but the heat wasn't in it. Johnny and I were both born here, but that didn't stop the assholes who hired him calling him 'Juan' or talking about him as if they thought he couldn't understand them. He kept his head down and his mouth shut, but the racist crap I heard about made my blood boil, and I was sure he left out the worst bits to keep me from going off like a volcano. That racist shit about Latina tempers is true, anyway.

'Did I hear he got that Carla girl pregnant?' Angelo asked, his voice a little more serious than usual.

I shrugged. 'Baby's a year old now. Little Cat.' Her name was Catalina, but no one called her that. 'He says he's gonna marry her when he can afford it, but I don't know.'

'Man, it's crazy the things you miss when you're away like that,' Angelo said. He leaned back and turned his gaze to the window, pensive. It made him look more mature, more sexy if that was possible.

I sighed and forced myself to turn back to the road and ignore his profile. His grin reappeared like magic as we pulled up to the halfway house and he snagged his duffel of clothes from the back seat. 'Wait here. Promise?'

'Yeah, whatever.' I leaned back in my own seat and left the car running. He'd stayed with Mrs Adams at least twice now, and even though she didn't trust him, I could tell she'd started to like him. Angelo had that devil's charm to him. A few minutes later he came jogging out the front door cackling like an idiot. From behind him I could hear Mrs Adams yelling at him in a steady stream, but he only jumped in the car and laughed.

'Well? Go on, hurry up!' He continued to laugh as she appeared in the front door, probably telling him he wasn't allowed to leave yet, though I couldn't hear her over his wild giggling.

'Stop it, would you? You sound like a little kid.' Plus the giggling was softening that part of me that I'd trained to firmly reject him. Him and the idea of taking my attraction to my favourite bad boy any farther than 'brother's buddy'.

'Did you see her face?' He laughed again, and I sighed at the big tattooed idiot giggling in my car.

When we got back to the house I was surprised to see that there weren't any cars in the driveway. Usually Carla was home, at least, but she must have gone out for groceries or to take Cat to the park. Johnny's truck was nowhere to be seen, either.

'Let's wait inside. I'm dying for some *cerveza*.'

'Are you supposed to drink?'

'No. What's your point?'

I followed him inside, and he wasted no time digging into the fridge for a cold beer. He passed one to me and popped the top on another, practically chugging the thing before I'd even taken two sips. 'Not thirsty, were you?' I asked. Where the hell was Johnny, anyway?

'Mama, it's been four years since I've had a beer, give me a fuckin' break.' He smiled to soften it, and I felt my knees go rubbery. I scowled at him and took a seat at the kitchen table to cover it.

'Johnny isn't here, so maybe you should go check in with your probation officer or whatever it is you're supposed to do. Wasn't Mrs Adams trying to get you to finish signing in or something?'

'Why you in such a hurry to get rid of me, girl? You're not afraid to be alone with old Angelo, are you?' He grinned and leaned in close to me, and I took a deep breath to steady myself before I could answer.

'I'm not afraid of you,' I said, trying not to stare into his dark brown eyes. His grin got wider, and he leaned over even more, his face only inches from mine.

'That's not what I asked you, mama,' he said, and then he crossed those last couple of inches and pressed his lips to mine. I moaned as his mouth made contact, and he teased my lips apart with his tongue almost immediately, explored my mouth and left behind the taste of beer. My heart thudded in my chest and my pussy felt like it was on fire.

The thud of a car door slamming made us jump apart, guiltily, and I leaped up and grabbed my beer before fleeing from the room. I made it to my bedroom before I heard the kitchen door bang open, and drank deeply as I listened to Johnny and Angelo greet each other like long-lost brothers, back in the kitchen. That was close. And stupid.

'And it is *not* happening again,' I muttered.

The next day was Saturday, and I had the day off from my job waitressing downtown. I slept in and woke sweaty and aroused from a dream of Angelo, so I was pretty grumpy when I made my way into the kitchen around lunchtime.

Carla was making sandwiches while my brother played with Cat, who was buckled into her high chair. 'What are you so happy about?' I asked him, glaring in response to the smile he gave me when I came in.

'Wow, who pulled your tail?'

'Sorry, I didn't sleep well. Is there any coffee left?' Of course not. I sighed and dug past the can of instant in the cabinet, wanting the good stuff. 'What are you guys up to?'

'Carla's just finishing up some lunch and we're going to take it to the park. You could come if you want,' he said, and I just caught the edge of Carla's irritation as she looked over her shoulder to glare at Johnny. She hated that I lived with them, but the truth was they couldn't afford the rent without me.

'Nah, I just want coffee and some quiet.' Cat squealed just then, and I made a playful face at her, causing her to giggle. Carla finished packing up the lunches and unstrapped the little girl from the high chair, and I waved

81

at them as they headed out through the kitchen door. The smell of the brewing coffee was starting to wake me up, at least.

I was halfway through my second cup when I heard tires crunch in the drive, and the sound of a radio cutting off. I tried very hard to pretend that I wasn't hoping it was Angelo, so I was almost surprised when his voice boomed out from behind me. "Sup, *chica?*'

'Don't you knock?' I said into the coffee cup. I took a sip to hide the thrill that went through me, knowing that we were here, again, alone. 'Johnny left, come back later.'

He swaggered around the table and poured himself a cup of my good coffee, and I glared at him as he sat down across from me with his usual disarming smile. 'Don't give me that look, baby, you know you're happy to see old Angelo at your door. Maybe I'm not here to see Johnny, eh?'

'Well, there's no one else here who might be interested to see you, so maybe next time you should just hit the Starbucks,' I said sweetly. He laughed, and the sound brought that familiar warmth back to the pit of my stomach. Why did he have to be so hot when he was so much trouble?

'You sure about that, mama?' His eyes were smouldering, and I had to take a deep breath, nearly choking on my coffee as he caught me off guard. The way he leaned across the table, he was like a restrained predator, and I felt myself grow slick with arousal at the thought of what he might do next.

'This is stupid,' I said breathily. Then I stood up, went around the table and straddled his lap. His arms came around me instantly, unsurprised, and his lips met mine with hungry, crushing force. I made a pleased sound at the back of my throat and crushed my breasts against him as I let the passion of the kiss overwhelm my senses. His beard scratched at my face and his hands dug into my back. My treacherous body responded with overwhelming approval.

When he pulled back a moment later, it was only to push my T-shirt up over my breasts. 'Nice jammies,' he teased, and I would have shot back that I'd have worn the good stuff if I had company worth sharing them with, but he shut me up by latching on to my nipple, sending a bolt of pleasure shooting through me. His mouth worked expertly at my breast and I wondered when, in all his time in and out of prison, he'd found the time to practise.

As he licked and sucked at my nipple, I grabbed the back of the chair and ground my hips against him, rubbing my pussy against his swollen cock. I could feel the hot, hard length of him through his jeans, rising up in reaction to me, and I realised that unless he'd had an adventure last night, this was going to be the first time in years that he'd had sex. I laughed at the power of that thought, and Angelo pulled back to cock an eyebrow at me. 'Something funny, princess?'

'Not at all,' I said, my voice as sweet and mocking as I could make it. He grabbed my hips and ground into me in response, then picked me up, bent forward, set me on the table and leaned over me.

'Glad to hear that,' he said, and he grabbed my pyjama pants, complete with cute little ducks and sheep, dragged them off over my hips and ass and tossed them into a corner of the kitchen. He plunged a finger into my wetness as he bent over me, watching my face, and I closed my eyes and threw my head back, wildly turned on. 'Damn, you're tight, mama,' he moaned.

I tried to tell myself that he was behaving like a barbarian and that he was no good for me and that we were on the fucking kitchen *table*, for Christ's sake, but none of that mattered. All I could concentrate on were the sensations of his lips on my collarbone, his huge paw of a right hand crushing my breast, and his other hand stroking me from the inside, making me crazy.

'I like that,' Angelo murmured above me. 'I like that wet hot pussy. You want me, baby?'

'God,' I moaned, 'do I have to say it?'

'Yeah, say it. Say, "Fuck me, Angelo." I want you to beg for it.' He was grinning as he pulled his finger away from me. He searched through his pockets until he came up with a condom, which he held in front of me like it was the key to all my desires.

'Fuck you, Angelo.'

He laughed and unfastened his pants. 'Close enough!' I reached for my clit as the little packet tore, and rubbed myself as I watched him roll the condom on over his straining erection. My entire body was on fire, and little waves of pleasure were already flowing through me as I anticipated what was to come. He poised himself over me, that stupid grin still on his face, and pushed inside.

I winced, just a little, at the pain of penetration, and Angelo froze, the smile gone from his face. This time it was my turn to grin at the shocked look he gave me. 'Was that –? Were you –? Ah, nah ... tell me I did *not* just deflower my man's little sister on his kitchen table.'

'Actually it's *my* kitchen table,' I said.

'Why you little ...' He was shaking his head, and his expression was unreadable.

'You gonna fuck me, or what?' As funny as this whole thing was, my cunt was still throbbing with arousal, and now that the pain was gone I just wanted *more*. My fingers continued their work on my clit, and I gasped as I got the angle just right.

His face slowly flooded with arousal again, and, when the hunger reached his eyes, Angelo leaned even farther over me, wrapped a fist in my hair and pressed the other hand on my hip with almost bruising strength as he pounded into me. I nearly screamed as the pleasure mounted, my fingers working furiously on my clit as his cock gave me new and exciting sensations to enjoy.

I let loose when I came, howling my pleasure to the empty house, and Angelo followed as my body milked his cock dry.

He pulled away a moment later, knotted the condom and tossed it in the kitchen trash. 'Damn, girl, that was hot. But what's that about, not telling me you're a virgin?'

'None of your business, was it, Romeo?' I asked, smirking. I wasn't sure who had come out on top in this scenario, but I was feeling satisfied and very, very pleased. And when I checked, there was no blood on the table. Good.

I gathered up my pyjama pants as Angelo pulled his jeans back up, and I made sure to give him a good view as I bent over for them. I started to leave the kitchen, and paused in the doorway. 'Of course, if you prefer more experienced women, you could always leave …'

As I'd hoped, he followed me to my bedroom. I tossed the bottoms to one side, and then pulled off my top and ditched it too. When I turned back to face him, the hungry look had returned to Angelo's eyes. 'Do you have another rubber in your pocket, or do I have to go steal one from my brother's bathroom?'

'Oh, man, do we have to even go there?'

'Well, you can only "deflower" a girl once, baby. So you wanna go again or not?' I backed up to the bed, climbed on and knelt with my legs spread wide and my pussy on display as I started to touch myself again.

It only took a second for Angelo to fish out another condom and pull his shirt over his head. He locked the door behind him and then crossed the room in a couple of quick strides before kicking out of his pants.

'Damn, girl, you're taking a walk on the wild side today. I like it ...' He gently pushed me back onto the bed and I went, spreading my legs as he speared me with two fingers. 'No wonder you're so fucking tight.' He moaned approval of my body, lowered his head and licked gently at my clit before nipping at the folds around it. I sighed as his tongue teased and caressed my body and, after a few minutes of that pleasant teasing, things got serious. His tongue began to work in earnest, and I twitched and writhed under his skilled touch as he fucked me with his fingers and teased me toward an orgasm.

When one last flick of the tongue sent me over the edge, I clamped my legs around his head and cried out in pleasure, my hands digging into his hair in my excitement. He continued to lick, teasing me until the intensity was more than I could bear and I thrust him away again. 'You're good at that,' I said.

'Practice makes perfect.' His cocky smile annoyed me for a moment.

'What, rimming guys in jail?' I smirked until I saw the glint that my comment brought to his eyes. He crawled up my body and pinned me to the bed, frightening me for a second with the intensity of his stare.

'You,' he said, 'are a bad girl.' Then he shifted his weight and pulled, moving off of me and rolling me onto his lap in one smooth motion, so fast I barely had time to register that I'd been moved before the first stinging swat on my ass. I screamed, but he kept it up and held me down, swatting in a steady rhythm that soon had me moaning and squirming more than fighting and screaming.

A small voice in my mind screamed that I was letting a man hit me, but I wasn't, really. He wasn't hitting, he was spanking, and even though it was something that I had never even considered, it was pushing all the right buttons for me now. I writhed against him, trying to get traction against my inflamed clit as he heated my backside.

I was startled a little later when the expected smack didn't come, but seconds after that he was plunging his fingers inside me again, then bringing my arousal to his mouth and licking it away. I rolled back over to watch him, and he grinned at me. 'Delicious,' he teased.

His hand dropped to his cock, which was hard again, and he began to stroke himself slowly, staring down at my body. I let him – I worked out and ate OK, and I was proud of my slender form and toned arms and legs. I was happy to lie back and let him look his fill as long as I got what I wanted in the end.

And I did. Eventually, it was him that broke, reaching

for the condom and slipping it on, then pushing my legs up over his shoulders and thrusting in deep and hard. He reached around and rubbed at my clit with his thumb, teasing me towards pleasure as he fucked me deep and slow. I came with a whimper and a moan, letting the pulsing of my body and the tension of my expression tell the story for me. The truth was, I was only so quiet because I was so busy soaring that I was too distracted to scream.

He waited a couple of seconds for me to recover, and I slowly came back to myself, still breathing hard, my eyes still slightly out of focus. Then he adjusted his angle and began to fuck me hard and fast, slamming into my sensitised body so that I screamed and bucked beneath him at the exquisite sensation. He buried himself in me as he came, moaning and calling out like the world was coming to an end before collapsing on the bed next to me.

He rested there for several long minutes, stroking my hair and my breasts. Then he got up, threw away the condom and started to get dressed.

'Are you leaving?' I asked.

He nodded. 'Better if Johnny doesn't know certain things.'

'You gonna come around again?'

He turned and gave me that charming smile. 'For you, mama? No question.' And then he left me there, naked on my bed. I heard the kitchen door slam a moment later, and sighed as I gathered up some clean clothes and went for a shower.

He didn't call the next day, or the next, and I started to get angry. I waited four days before I casually brought his name up in conversation with my brother.

'I thought I told you,' he said, shaking his head. 'Moron wasn't out a week before someone called the cops on him for burglarising some place in the 'burbs. It was – what? – three, four days ago?'

I shook my head and bent over my lunch, trying not to let anything show on my face. I had thought I would be upset, but in truth I was relieved. It had been a hot experience and the fulfilment of a lot of years of teenage fantasy, but Angelo was trouble, and if he stayed in my life it was only going to get complicated, fast.

Angelo Ramirez was a dangerous dalliance – he could never be anything else.

Paying My Way
Lucy Salisbury

Did I dare? That was the great question. I was sure it was practical, and if I wasn't sure exactly what might happen, then that was half the fun. It was also safe, at least in so far as I had plenty of time and there was no reason whatsoever that anybody who mattered would find out. Whether I was safe in the sense of being likely to get to Paris with my virtue intact was a different matter entirely, but then that was the whole point. But did I dare?

The idea was simple. I would get off the train at Calais, and instead of continuing to Paris on the TGV I would make my way into town. I'd then seek out a café or a bar where the long-distance truck drivers gathered, choose the biggest, roughest, dirtiest-looking bastard I could find and trade the use of my body for a lift to Paris, or at least in that general direction. There were one or two technical drawbacks, such as finding the right man in the right lorry, but the shame and embarrassment of doing so would make the experience all the stronger. I also had to be sure he'd take me up on my offer, because it would be bitterly frustrating to set off and end up being dropped off unmolested.

I'd even made my preparations in advance, sending my luggage on ahead and dressing more or less as I had when I was a student, so that, hopefully, I'd look like a good prospect for sex but not worth stealing from. That meant skin-tight jeans, little fur-lined boots, a top and a jumper, with several spare pairs of knickers in my shoulder bag. My hair was up in a high pony-tail, a style I knew from experience allowed me to pass for eighteen, while my make-up and scent were both a little bolder than I'd have used in the office. I carried a single debit card, carefully concealed, along with a handful of Euros.

After taking so much trouble I knew I'd feel like a fool if I backed out, but it still took courage just to abandon the Eurostar and make my way into Calais. I knew where to go, more or less, and was growing ever more nervous as my surroundings became increasingly rough. My arousal was growing too, with the thoughts of what might happen to me and what I might be made to do becoming ever more vivid. By the time I got to the big truckstop I'd identified on the Internet from the safety of my flat the night before, I was shaking and struggling to keep up the confident smile that was essential to my plans. I need to look like easy pickings for some over-sexed bastard, not a frightened little girl whom even the most rampant trucker was likely to take straight to the police.

It worked. There were a dozen or so men seated outside the crude bar near the gates, each and every one as rough and unashamedly masculine as I could possibly have hoped for. As I approached, heads began to turn and comments were passed, setting me blushing. I'd already decided it would be best to speak only schoolgirl French, making me seem more vulnerable still while allowing me to keep up with what was going on.

'Is anyone going towards Paris?'

There was an immediate ripple of conversation among them, shrugs, expressions of regret. I'd hoped to get several volunteers and choose between them, picking out the one who seemed most likely to demand sex in payment for the trip and, if he proved to be a gentleman after all, offering myself in payment. As it was, all of them seemed to be heading the other way, across the Channel or north towards Belgium and the Netherlands. I asked again.

'Paris? The south maybe?'

Again there was a ripple of conversation among them, before one pointed a dirty finger towards the ranked lorries.

'Lantier, there.'

I could see the Lantier lorry, a grubby canvas-sided trailer with a red cab, just the sort I'd imagined in my frequent fantasies. Now it was real, and my heart was hammering in my chest as I made my way across. There were several drivers hanging around the lorries, talking amongst themselves. Again they saw me coming, and again my appearance provoked immediate interest, setting my nipples hard as I imagined what they'd do if I found myself having to entertain all of them together. It wasn't at all obvious which one belonged to my vehicle, forcing me to ask once again.

'Lantier? To Paris, perhaps towards the south?'

One of them stepped out from among the others and I felt my knees go weak. He was massive, only a little taller than me but with huge shoulders, the bulging muscles showing even beneath his heavy donkey jacket. His arms had to be as thick as my legs and his chest was like a barrel, his belly and hips thick and hard, all encased in grubby, oil-smeared workman's blues. A bristling blond beard adorned his rounded face, while there was no mistaking the import of his grin, nor the look in his pale-grey eyes. I was going to get it, and then some.

'Lantier?'

'Yes, to Nyons.'

'Noyon, good.'

I'd answered him, but I'd barely heard, already

imagining myself being made to suck his cock in return for my lift, at the very least. Not only that, but Noyon would leave me short of my destination and I might find myself obliged to get a second lift, or bribe him to make a detour, which was sure to really cost me. All it needed was for me to close the deal, but with over a dozen truckers looking at me and exchanging knowing smiles and smutty remarks I found myself at a loss for what to say. My driver cocked a thumb at his massive chest.

'Claude.'

'Lucy. Hello. I'm English.'

He responded with a nod, then tapped his watch.

'Sixteen hours.'

It was only just after three, which left me with nearly an hour before we set off. I smiled and nodded my understanding, but it was a problem I hadn't really considered. In my fantasies they'd have passed the time by sharing me between them, perhaps spread naked in the back of some ancient van with a mattress on the floor as they took turns with me, or even forced me to scamper from cab to cab in nothing but my boots, with my boobs bouncing and my bare bottom jiggling behind me to the sound of their coarse laughter. They obviously liked me, and envied Claude, but I couldn't see them being that mean. I was beginning to feel muddled, and the only thing I could think of to do was to point to his cab.

'May I sit in the lorry, please?'

'Sure.'

He walked me across and as we went I caught a remark from the men behind us, something about the way my bottom moved as I walked, then laughter. I went red, and redder still as another man spoke, in thickly accented French, calling out to Claude to tell him he was a lucky guy. When we reached the lorry Claude opened the door and for a moment his hand was on my bottom as he boosted me up. I thought my moment had come, that he'd follow and start to touch me up, with a straight choice of surrender or getting kicked out of the cab, but he slammed the door behind me and walked away.

I slumped back in the seat, my eyes closed, my hands shaking. He'd touched my bottom. One of his mates had at least implied that I ought to be good for sex. I wanted it, badly, even if only to rip down my jeans and panties and bring myself off under my fingers, but I was sure I'd be getting much more than that, if only I showed a little patience. Claude hadn't gone back to the others, but was walking towards the bar, to disappear inside and emerge with a steaming mug in each hand. I opened the door for him as he reached the lorry, smiling my gratitude as I reached down for what turned out to be soup. He walked around to climb in on the other side, grinning and giving me a thumbs-up before starting to blow on his soup. I waited, praying he'd proposition me, feeling utterly ridiculous and deeply

96

ashamed of myself and as horny as a she-cat in heat all at the same time.

He made no move, but held the mug in his huge, rough hands and sipped his soup. I watched sidelong, imagining those big hands on my body, hauling my top up to get at my breasts, fumbling at my nipples, his coarse, hard skin against the softness of my flesh as he enjoyed me. Still he sat and drank his soup, only to suddenly turn on me, grinning like a polecat. My heart seemed to leap up into my mouth and I felt the muscles of my sex contract as if I was about to come, but he turned away again, perhaps unsure of his English, or that I'd understand his French. I gave him an encouraging smile and he tried again.

'You are student?'

It wasn't what I'd been hoping for, but it gave me an opening.

'Yes. A student. Very poor.'

He gave a glum nod, but the last thing I needed was his sympathy.

'I am sorry,' I tried, 'but I have no money for petrol, er ... gasoil.'

He began to say something in English, thought better of it and reverted to French.

'It's not a worry. The company pays.'

'I should pay.'

'No, no.'

'No, really, I mean I haven't got any money, but –'

97

'It's not a worry, really.'

I was going to have to say it myself.

'I mean, to pay … for my ride. I would like to … like to … oh God, how do you say it in French? What's "to suck"? Er … put your penis in my mouth … please?'

My face felt as if it was on fire, blazing with shame, but I'd done it. He was looking at me, uncertain, before giving the most Gallic of shrugs, putting his soup down and reaching into his workman's blues to pull out a big, grubby-looking cock and a set of extraordinarily hairy balls. For a moment I could only stare, wondering how I could possibly want to go anywhere near the grotesque thing, let alone suck it, but then I did exactly that, leaning over to take hold and pop him into my mouth. He tasted of oil and man but, for all that my face had screwed up in automatic disgust, the heartfelt moan that had escaped my throat expressed pure bliss.

I was doing it, sucking cock for a lorry driver to pay him for a lift, something I'd fantasised over more often than I could remember. It was heavenly, leaving me weak with emotion as he began to stir in my mouth, and completely vulnerable as he moved a hand to my chest. He began to feel my breasts, groping me through my jumper as his cock got slowly longer and fatter. I let him, telling myself I ought to be a good girl and do my best to keep him happy. My hand went to his balls and I began to squeeze and stroke, then to masturbate him into my mouth.

At that he began to pull up my top clothes, perhaps realising that I didn't actually feel obliged at all, but that he'd caught a dirty little bitch. I sucked more eagerly still, rolling his meaty foreskin back with my lips in a deliberately dirty gesture as my boobs came bare. He began to grope me again, and to moan with pleasure as his rough hands explored the contours of my chest. I took him deep, deliberately making myself gag on the head of his cock, then a second time. He gasped and called me a slut, his free hand closed in my hair, and any chance I had of escape was gone as he began to fuck my mouth.

I just took it, helpless in his grip as he used me, his now stiff cock pushing in and out between my lips as he fumbled at my naked breasts. It was perfect, my top up in a lorry cab as I was forced to suck the driver's cock, his grip tight in my hair, my jaw aching as he pumped into my mouth. When he did pull me up it was just to wank for a moment, and perhaps show off his cock, now a long dirty-pink pole of man-flesh, taut in erection and glistening with my spit.

For a moment I thought he was going to deliberately spunk in my face, then I was pushed back down. As my mouth filled with cock once more I was half wishing he'd done it, even though I was equally keen to be made to swallow, but the real joy lay in having no choice. It didn't matter what I wanted. He was going to have his fun with me the way he liked, which was to jam his cock as deep into my throat as it would go, with his fist twisted hard in my hair and his other hand squeezing his balls as he gave me his full load.

I was very nearly sick, and it left me with my eyes watering and bubbles of spunk blowing from my nose, but I managed to swallow most of it before he allowed me to pull back. For a moment I was gasping for breath, but I couldn't resist the sight of his messy cock and stayed down to lick up what remained from his shaft. He called me a slut again, but he was grinning as I finally sat back in my seat to adjust my clothes, and so was I.

'I am yours, until Noyon. Is that fair?'

He gave a happy nod, then twisted around to take a box of tissues from behind the little curtain that closed off the area behind the seats. I could guess what they were for, cleaning his cock when he masturbated, which added a fresh touch of humiliation as I wiped my nose and lips. A glance in the mirror showed that my make-up had run, making me look a bit of a clown, so I burrowed into my bag to make the necessary adjustments. Claude had gone back to his soup, not even bothering to put his cock away until he'd refreshed himself.

We left shortly afterwards, Claude driving with practised ease to bring us out onto the motorway, where he settled down to a steady speed. I was horny but relaxed, knowing he was sure to take advantage of my offer in due course, while much of the pleasure of the fantasy lay in having him make the choices. Sucking him off had been nice, especially once he'd begun to be forceful with me, but until that moment I'd been calling the shots. It had also been deliciously humiliating to have to ask him for what I needed, but it would have been better still for him to insist on his blowjob, my only alternative being left stranded in Calais.

As we drove south I was hoping he'd stop at some lonely rest area and demand more, perhaps even to fuck me. Yet he seemed content, silent most of the time, save for the occasional question, and not once mentioning that I'd just sucked him off. Before long my frustration had begun to grow once more, until I was wondering if I wouldn't have to force the issue for a second time. We passed Arras and turned onto the A1, the light now beginning to fade. I told myself that I was being greedy and that he'd need to recharge his balls before he could take proper advantage of me, that he might even wait until we got to Noyon, but as we passed a sign showing the approach of another rest area he began to slow the lorry. We had plenty of fuel, and the Aire de Maurepas advertised no facilities beyond parking, which could only mean one thing. I felt my belly start to tighten as Claude steered the lorry off the motorway, and he'd no sooner parked than he was grinning at me and using his thumb to indicate the little curtained-off area behind us.

'In the back. Clothes off.'

I was being told to strip, for sex, and it was perfect. At last I was going to get what I really deserved, a good rough fuck at the hands of a man who expected to use me as he pleased. I hesitated, hoping he'd give me another dirty, curt order, or at least a warning look to hint at what would happen if I didn't obey, abandoned on the roadside in the middle of nowhere. All he did was jerk his thumb towards the curtains a second time, a touch more aggressively, but that was enough. I scrambled over the seats, presenting my bottom as I crawled into the gloomy, warm cubicle and getting the pat of his hand I wanted across my seat.

The space was low and narrow, just big enough to hold a mattress and a tangle of blankets and sheets. He'd left a pornographic magazine to one side, some Dutch thing of the crudest possible sort, showing brassy women with their legs spread wide to show off the pink insides of their cunts or working on huge, virile cocks. A powerful shudder ran through me as I pushed it further back. It was easy to imagine him getting his big brown cock off over the cheap, dirty pictures, but this time he wasn't going to need it, because he had me and I'd be treated just the same, cheap and dirty.

He was making a good start, with the curtain pulled back a little so that he could watch me undress. It was impossible to be elegant about it, let alone teasing, with the roof so close above me and barely enough room to turn over. I pulled my jumper and top off to go bare-breasted once more, took off my boots and pushed down my jeans and socks, to leave me in nothing but panties. Not that they were staying up anyway, but as I threw everything else onto the seat he made a small peremptory gesture, indicating that I should get them off too. If there's one thing I love it's being told to get out of my panties by a strong, eager lover, and I wriggled out of them in a second, tossed them onto the rest of my clothes and left myself nude. He took a while to admire my body before reaching out to touch me, his calloused fingers moving on my flesh as if to marvel over how smooth and soft I was.

I moved in a little to make room for him. He climbed up and pawed me with rising urgency. I did my best to respond, letting him kiss me and putting an arm around his massive shoulders as he squashed in next to me. He was rough, squeezing my breasts and bottom, thrusting one big finger up my cunt and then simply mounting me. I let my thighs spread wide, accepting him although his weight was crushing me, and as he began to fumble with the fly of his workman's blues I knew that I'd well and truly fulfilled my fantasy. He was going to fuck me, and there was nothing I could do about it.

I felt his cock as he pulled it free, hot against my thigh, then his fist smacking on my flesh as he hurriedly wanked himself to erection while he kissed and suckled at my breasts. As his cock began to swell he pushed it between the lips of my cunt, rubbing in my slit with his helmet, his fingers bumping on my clitoris and over my lips to leave me gasping and shaking my head in mingled pleasure and pain. He pulled my legs up, spreading me wider still, pressed his cock to my hole and he was up, forcing himself in with three good shoves before taking me under my shoulders and ramming himself the rest of the way in. I clung on as my fucking continued, with his full weight on my naked body, my thighs cocked painfully wide, his big cock pumping hard in my cunt.

He took his time over me, first on top, then turning me over and making me stick my bottom up so that he could mount me from the rear, pulling me on top of him so that he could play with my tits while I rode his body, and finally putting me on my back once more before whipping his cock free and straddling my face to fuck my mouth for a second time. I was made to swallow again and then just left, naked and bruised in his makeshift bed, my body sore and sticky, my cunt desperately in need of the touch of my fingers.

I did it openly, masturbating in front of the man who just given me a rough, dirty fuck in exchange for a lift, and as my body locked in orgasm he gave me the perfect accolade, calling me a slut one more time. With that I was done, my energy gone, my body used, but both satisfied and triumphant at the same time. I'd really done it, in

fine style, living a fantasy I'd enjoyed for so long despite
all the restrictions of my day-to-day life. He didn't seem
that bothered, which was just as it should have been.
He simply passed me the tissues and sat back into his
seat. We were soon moving again, but I stayed as I was,
cuddled nude into the warm blankets and quickly falling
into a drowsy, contented sleep.

We were still on the motorway when I woke up again. It
was pitch-black outside, with only the occasional distant
yellow twinkle to mark buildings. There was far less
traffic too: nobody ahead of us and only a scattering
of headlights coming the other way. That seemed odd,
when we were presumably getting fairly close to Paris,
and then a big square sign loomed out of the darkness.
It showed a building roofed with fantastically coloured
tiles and bore a single word, 'Beaune'.

'Where are we?'

Claude turned, grinning.

'Halfway. More. Soon we stop again.'

He gave me a slow, greasy wink, which I ignored.

'That sign said Beaune. That's in Burgundy!'

He gave one his shrugs.

'Of course.'

'We shouldn't be in Burgundy! I'm supposed to be
going to Paris, Noyon anyway.'

'Nyons, yes. Halfway.'

He reached into a shelf to pull out a clipboard, which

he passed back. I could hardly see it in the dim light, but it was plainly a map of France, with a long, irregular line drawn across it, ending in a circle by which somebody had scrawled the name of his destination, Nyons. It was somewhere in the Alps.

'Oh God! Look, stop, as soon as you can!'

'We stop soon, pretty girl.'

'No, I mean, I have to get out!'

'You need make pee-pee?'

'No ... yes ... anything, just stop!'

He laughed.

'What a slut, but it is good.'

As he spoke another sign loomed up, showing the junction between two motorways. We soon pulled off, to a huge lorry park lit by high, bright lights, where I had no choice but to suck his cock one more time. I did enjoy it, but my mind wasn't really on the task in hand, but on how to get back to Paris, which was now at least as far as it had been from Calais, but in the opposite direction. I had my debit card, but I had no idea where the station was or if any trains would be running in the dead hours of the night.

On the other hand, there were plenty of lorries around, and plenty of drivers.

Looking for Lance
Tenille Brown

Lance wasn't the type to call and check in, so Regina wasn't going to fool herself. There was no need to sit at home and wait and think that maybe, just maybe, in the middle of the night she'd hear a knock on the door and there he'd be with a dozen roses in his hands, grinning.

That just wasn't Lance's way.

His way was fucking Regina hard, rough and steady during the middle of a thunderstorm, leaving her with a bleeding bottom lip and sore and purple pussy, and then disappearing for days and weeks at a time before reappearing again.

But Regina tended to get restless in the meantime and she couldn't help that.

So she did what she could.

Take tonight, for instance. She pulled a ten from her

bra and handed it over to the bouncy, top-heavy dancer who squirmed and writhed in front of her.

Jade – she had repeated her name over and over to Regina like the chorus of a song – snatched the money up and tucked it into the lace garter hugging her thigh.

'Two for one for the next fifteen minutes,' Jade said. 'For you, sexy, we'll make it three for one.'

'That's cool,' Regina said and leaned back in the uncomfortable vinyl chair.

Jade wasn't extremely pretty. She wasn't even what Regina would call sexy, but Regina closed her eyes and leaned back anyway and imagined that Lance was in a corner in this club somewhere watching it all go down between the two of them.

Lance had a thing for girl-on-girl action, though he liked to pretend he didn't. He was much too macho for that.

But Regina could tell by the way he always seemed to pump faster and harder when they were watching porn and one chick was eating another chick's cunt. His nails would drag down her back and he'd be so engrossed in the two women on the screen that he wouldn't even hear Regina's screams or realise that she had become so wet that his cock could hardly stay inside.

This place where Jade was giving Regina dirty dances was a dingy little dive she had stumbled upon, and it was precisely Lance's type of spot. It was in one of the rougher parts of town, where Regina wouldn't normally go, except that tonight she couldn't convince herself to stay at home.

The music thumped through the speakers clamped to the sweating walls.

Jade bounced and shook in front of Regina in her cobalt-blue bikini.

This place didn't even have a 'no-touch' rule.

So Jade touched Regina and Regina touched Jade.

Jade had clearly grown attached to Regina over this last hour and, after the third song ended, she invited her to the Champagne Room. The privilege didn't come without a price, but Regina had slipped far beyond reason. Once the door was closed behind them, she pulled her small roll of bills from her bra, picked off the requested amount and pressed it into Jade's hands.

'Now ... what can I do for you, baby?' Jade asked, placing her platform-heeled foot on the gaudy ottoman in front of Regina.

But Regina knew that tonight's special request wasn't to eat or be eaten, so she shook her head.

No, she wanted to whet her appetite in another way altogether.

Regina leaned forward in her seat. She asked, as confidently as she could, 'How do you feel about spanking, Miss Jade?'

Then she stood up and straightened her fitted jacket.

Jade shrugged. 'I don't judge anyone. And I don't have many rules. Just no bruises, OK? This body is how I make my money.'

'No, Jade, honey,' Regina said. 'I was wondering if *you* would like to spank *me*?'

It sounded funny as only a suggestion, not the begging she was used to with Lance. She would whimper and grovel for hours before he would give in. But that, Regina knew, was what made it all worth it, when Lance finally gave her what she asked for, the pain followed by the ecstasy.

A smile spread across Jade's plain golden face. 'Well, that's no problem, sweetie. Just pull 'em down and bend that tight ass right on over.'

Regina obeyed.

'Just make it hurt,' she said as she slid down her black leather pants. She knelt on the red suede sectional, pressed her head against the back of it and waited, bracing herself for what was sure to come.

Like a strike of lightning was the palm of Jade's hand on her left ass cheek. With her fair complexion, Regina knew that alone was enough to bruise.

Jade was using her hand, the only tool at her disposal, but at this moment it was enough for Regina. Jade reached far back and brought her palm down hard on Regina's soft cheeks, and Regina knew the customers in the main area could hear the slapping coming from the small room in the back.

Doing what she was used to, Jade spanked Regina in time to the music that was steadily pumping through the walls and the closed and locked door.

The spanking lasted two, then three songs, until the lyrics and the rhythm became a blur in Regina's mind and all she could hear was the steady *smack, smack* of hand on ass.

Her ass was so sore now that tears sprang to her clenched eyes. But she hadn't found it yet, what she was looking for, that thing that Lance gave so effortlessly, and the more Jade spanked and Regina's ass jiggled in response, the more she knew there was a very good chance she wouldn't find it here.

The spanking was slowing down, and now and then Regina caught Jade stopping to rub the palm of her hand.

'Time's up,' Jade said after the fourth song ended.

Regina found herself more relieved than satisfied, but she tipped plain Jade anyway and slipped her tongue inside her pouty mouth.

'Thank you, doll,' Regina said, before she left the Champagne Room and the dingy club for the night.

* * *

Regina didn't know why she was still awake. She had watched her favourite porno and used her dildo tonight and had come thirty minutes ago.

It had been satisfying enough. After all, *she* knew what she liked.

Still, she lay there like a lonely and impatient wife, waiting for her husband to come home from work.

She looked over at the phone on the nightstand that she knew wouldn't ring.

Had Lance *ever* called and asked to come over?

Of course not.

Lance never asked permission to do anything, to come over, to come inside of her, to jerk off while standing over Regina and come on her skin, her lips, her hair.

Lance tended to just appear, give Regina what he seemingly knew she was dying for, and then he was gone just as quickly as he came.

Regina turned over again and flipped her pillow, sighing.

She remembered she had cried the first time Lance fucked her. She never told anyone that.

It had been partly because of the pain of his thickness filling her shallow cunt, but mostly from the pleasure of being mashed tightly against him, his raspy voice growling word after nasty word in her ear as he pounded her.

They had fucked on the cold, wet ground behind a closed drugstore. It had happened even though Regina had told herself that they were just going for a ride and that was all. She wouldn't just give it up so easy.

But he had said a word, maybe two, and suddenly she was a mere paperclip drawn to his magnet and she was fucking a virtual stranger in a place with no windows and no doors and she liked it.

Loved it, even.

Lance had called her beautiful. Said she smelled nice. Told her no one had ever listened to him the way she did. Regina *got* him and he rarely found that in a broad.

Sometimes Regina thought that was what did it. She had given Lance too much, too soon. Maybe that tear falling from her cheek to his shoulder was their defining moment and the tone was set for their relationship right then and there.

Regina realised that she was biting down on her bottom lip and it had begun to bleed on her pillow. She wiped it away with the back of her hand, reached into her nightstand and pulled out another dildo, this one almost the length and girth of Lance's cock, and slipped it under her sheets.

Regina closed her eyes and let her knees fall open. She didn't bother with lube because she wanted to feel every inch. She wanted to feel herself pull and stretch until the rubber cock was fully inside her, shaking and throbbing, and her cunt was swollen and aching, ready to come.

But even after she came, the aching realisation that a dildo couldn't give her what she wanted, what she needed from Lance, made her toss it aside.

She was sure Lance hadn't meant to spoil her, and he had made it clear to her in the beginning that he wasn't the relationship type of guy. If he hadn't come right out and said it, then he'd shown it with the way he never called and barely answered when Regina did.

And Regina was sure Lance never looked for her to become so accustomed to what they had, but something inside her urged her to claim him, to dig her nails in, hold on for dear life and call him hers.

How could he expect someone to become addicted to the twisted mess that was their relationship?

Was it love? Regina couldn't be sure but she knew she loved some things about Lance. She knew that she loved the smooth skin on the top of his head, and she loved the slight Jamaican accent that was still present even though he hadn't lived on the island for ten years.

She loved his fingers digging into her ass and slipping into her pussy. She even loved his scent. He didn't wear cologne. He wasn't with that pretty-boy shit. And most times he didn't even smell sweet. He smelled of the grimy streets he travelled late at night, making his hustles.

Those were all the things that attracted her to Lance. That was what kept her coming, kept her chasing, kept her looking.

But, knowing she wouldn't find him tonight, Regina finally fell asleep with the palm of her hand wedged between her legs, and flashes of Lance's face bouncing behind her eyelids.

* * *

Tonight, five weeks after the Jade episode, Regina had craved Lance and, as much as she told herself she wouldn't, she went looking for him anyway.

She had found him after only an hour and a half, at a raunchy club not three miles from her house. There in a corner she had seen him sitting beneath the perfectly spread haunches of a wide-hipped dancer.

Sweating – he'd been sweating like he was doing the hardest work of his life when really he was just sitting there while a young woman who called herself Jovial worked, grinding, lifting, dropping.

Regina had snatched him up after a few minutes more, pulled him out of there by the collar of his shirt.

'Follow me.'

Lance cocked his head. 'Follow you where?'

He was angry.

Regina didn't care. In fact, she liked it.

'My house,' she said.

Even now, driving like there were no curves in the road, Regina didn't know where she had mustered the nerve, how she knew Lance wouldn't snatch away or even push her to the ground in anger.

Maybe he had been missing her, too.

Turning into her driveway, Lance close behind her, Regina wondered again what it was, why she never could stop looking.

Maybe it was the allure of the unattainable, maybe

she was some sort of masochist, but every time, Regina came back for more. She sought him out, pushed his buttons until he gave her what she wanted. Only then was she satisfied, only then could she again think like a sensible and sane person.

They stumbled inside the house but didn't even make it to the bedroom. Instead they fell onto the floor just inside the corridor, landing next to the coatrack. Regina was on top of Lance, but only briefly before he rolled her over so that she was pinned beneath him.

'Take my pants off,' Regina begged, writhing and bucking her hips. But it was as if she had said nothing at all because Lance only pressed his knee between her thighs, forcing them apart.

He was grinding against her, cock rock-hard, clothes still on. Lance was making Regina wet and bringing fitful tears to her eyes.

She reached up and with all her strength brought his velvety black face down to hers.

It didn't matter if Lance kissed her or not, she just wanted to feel his lips somewhere, anywhere, so he placed them on her neck, rubbing them roughly against the delicate skin before he bit down hard.

Regina's back arched in pain.

Lance half-smiled. 'You like that, then.'

Regina nodded.

Lance stood up and pulled off his white T-shirt so

that he was wearing only a wife-beater and his khaki pants.

It didn't matter at this point. Regina didn't need to see him fully naked. It didn't matter whether he stripped down and showed her that beautifully built body of his or removed not one piece of clothing. She didn't even care if Lance asked her to get out of her own clothes, or if he tore them off her body in a frenzy.

She just wanted to feel him. She just had to have him inside her.

It didn't matter that when he finally crouched down again, the only part of Lance that touched her was his cock. He bore his weight on his arms as he hovered above her, giving himself to Regina in pumps, rises and falls.

This, this was what Regina had been looking for, waiting for, begging for.

Lance used his knees to spread Regina's legs farther, as wide as they would go.

Regina welcomed him. She welcomed him into the centre of her, a void that only he could fill.

'Ride me,' Lance demanded. And just like that he turned them into the position.

Regina rode Lance while fidgeting with her clothes. After a while her bra was half loose and she had only one earring on. Somewhere in the tussle her necklace had popped in two.

But suddenly Lance held Regina still. 'I'm not ready,' he said. He leaned up and sucked roughly on Regina's nipples.

It stung and it satisfied her. Regina swayed between screaming and giggling, but she did neither as Lance inserted his index finger into her anus.

Regina rose off Lance's hips just enough that he could finger her properly. Then she reached down and cupped her breasts, suspended on his cock, enjoying his finger, waiting for the OK to begin fucking him again.

Finally Lance said, 'Now go. Go hard and make me come.'

Regina lifted up so high and came down so hard she made it hurt. It hurt so good she couldn't even look at Lance any more.

She didn't see him when he came, when he hit her directly in the chest with his hot semen. Covered in Lance's pearl-white wetness, she tumbled off of him and lay on her back on the cold tile, spent.

'So. Did you find what you were looking for?' he asked, pulling his shorts and then his khaki pants back on.

Regina nodded.

'Good,' he said.

It was on the tip of her tongue to invite him to the bedroom, to ask him to stay so that they could have breakfast in bed in the morning, but she knew better.

So she lay there, asking instead, 'Are you coming back?'

Lance looked down at Regina's half-naked body and licked his lips. 'Yeah. I'll be back.'

* * *

Regina almost didn't stop. But the heartbeat-like thumping of the music coming from inside the club made her manoeuvre her car into the parking lot and walk inside.

Standing just inside the door, she watched bodies grinding close. It made her want to grab someone herself and do some grinding of her own.

'I like the way you move ...' The song vibrated the speakers and incited sweat from the many people who swayed back and forth to its rhythm.

The club was called Slide. It was small and comfortably crowded, wall-to-wall full of regulars who frequented the spot because either they were loyal or they just wanted a night of low-key partying: drink a little, dance a little, go home and get a little.

Regina hadn't particularly been in the mood to party and she wasn't craving a drink but, since she was here, she supposed could go for a dance.

In the middle of the floor next to no one in particular, her hips moved. Regina shifted from side to side effortlessly in her high heels. Her calves flexed as she dipped low and twisted her way back up.

In her short red dress with the ruffles on the hem she

119

thought she might be overdressed, but a slight glance over her shoulder let her know that he was there, standing in a corner, watching her.

Regina turned her back to him and shook her ass in his direction. She felt the ruffles rise and knew her red lace panties were showing. She also knew he wasn't the only one who could see.

She wondered how hard he'd work to beat the others to the punch.

She knew what she had come here for. Regina knew just what she was looking for, what she was always looking for.

When the club was empty except for her, him and the DJ, he put on a CD and started to clean up.

Prince was thumping from the twin speakers. 'Soft and wet,' he sang in his notorious falsetto.

Finally, he dropped the cloth he was using to wipe tables and walked over to her. Regina didn't wait to see what he would do. As of tonight, she was tired of waiting.

She reached out and grabbed him. He hesitated, surprised, so she lifted her skirt.

It was enough to make him teeter in the other direction as if he was considering walking away. He looked around before grabbing her by the waist and leading her inside the bathroom.

His eyes dimmed at the sight of her tearing off her own panties and tossing them aside. He tugged nervously on his beard at the sight of the black patch of curly hair that was the only barrier between him and her pussy.

Soon the barrier was broken when he loosened his leather belt and let his black trousers slide down his legs onto the scummy bathroom floor.

Regina sighed in relief when he entered her. The bathroom was empty and silent except for her gasping and his grunting and the swoosh-swoosh smacking sound her wet pussy made as he pushed his cock in and out of her.

He balanced himself with his hands on the counter surrounding the triple sinks, leaning over her and pressing her ass firmly into the counter too.

He fucked her in shallow thrusts as if he were afraid to come too far out, as if he would lose some of what he was feeling if he got too far away.

Regina didn't mind. She opened her legs farther, stretched them open so wide that needle-point pains tickled her hips.

He kept looking in the mirror, cocky motherfucker, looking at himself and then looking at Regina, looking at himself while he fucked her, twisted grin on his face like he was enjoying the show their reflection was putting on.

He grabbed her roughly by the waist, holding her pinned against the mirror and the counter.

Another Prince song switched on in the background. 'You sexy motherfucker,' he wailed.

Soon there was sweat dripping off his black body

and onto hers. His fingers were intertwined in her kinky twisted hair, gathering it in his palm and then he was pulling.

Regina loved that shit. She especially loved that he could see the combination of pleasure and pain in her eyes and pulled harder.

Her legs were high in the air, her thighs gripping what she could of his meaty torso. His pants and briefs were down around his ankles, his boots providing the grip required to fuck in cramped quarters.

The sinks were rocking beneath their weight. The mirror directly behind her was shaking. Regina's head rocked back and forth as he forced his cock in and out of her cunt, grunting, growling and biting as he fucked her.

Then Regina's head landed hard and square against the bathroom mirror, cracking it instantly, then shattering it into pieces that fell to the floor.

He didn't stop or even hesitate. Regina wasn't sure he even saw or heard it, he was so engrossed in fucking her cunt.

Regina wrapped her legs around him tight, squeezing his cock with all she had until ...

'I'm ... about to ... *come*!' He shouted the words.

Regina knew as much, so with all the energy she had left she pushed him back, hopped off the sink and fell to her knees in front of him.

She took his rigid dick, slopping wet with her juices, into her mouth and began to suck. She didn't need to look up, didn't need to gaze into his face for reassurance. Regina knew what would make his legs tremble and his arms reach forward for support. She knew just what to do to make him shake like a spin cycle and throw his head back, bite his bottom lip hard and come, thick and hot against the back of her throat.

Regina took him in far enough to make herself gag. Then she swallowed. She found that his seed wasn't as sweet as she was used to.

She rose to her feet and ran a hand across the cracked surface of the bathroom mirror. She said, 'Sorry,' though she wasn't the one who had broken it, but she was used to apologising and over-accommodating.

And she was apologising though she wanted to thank him for the cuts she knew were on her back, for the pain that she knew would last at least a week or more.

That was Lance's fault.

'No worries,' he said, trying to catch his breath, 'I'll replace the mirror. Just promise me I get to fuck you like that again.'

And there it was, their defining moment.

She shook her head slowly as she put on her skirt and attempted to check herself in the broken mirror.

'*I* can replace the mirror ... Doug? Was that your name? And I'm sorry, but you won't get to fuck me again.'

123

Doug, the owner of Slide, cocked his head, confused. 'What, no next time?'

Regina shook her head again, replaced what she could of her clothes and left Doug standing there, half-naked and confused.

* * *

Her hair brushed and gelled into a sharp Mohawk, her body wrapped in a vinyl cat suit, Regina stepped out of her car.

She had parked at the very end of a dark alley, fully aware that it might be there when she was done and it might not. At this point it didn't matter. Regina had other things on her mind.

She walked the quarter-mile or so to the back entrance of the invitation-only dig she had found while surfing the Internet a few nights ago.

Standing at the top of the stairs and looking down at the moving bodies below, she thought the place had Lance written all over it.

Regina's lips were shiny with gloss. Her nipples were already hard. Her cunt was throbbing and primed for being fucked. She hoped it would happen tonight, with or without Lance.

She was looking for Lance again, though she hadn't found him in three months. She had combed the clubs, the gambling houses and the street corners.

And tomorrow, next week, next year, she knew, she'd be looking for Lance still.

A Night in with the Boys
Victoria Blisse

'I thought you were out,' he said, by way of an excuse for being caught with his mate's cock in his hand.

'I was but Natalie felt sick and Debbie took her home and I wasn't going to stay out on my own. So I'm back. I did ring but you didn't answer. Looks like you had your hands full.'

Really full actually. I couldn't stop staring at Luke's dick. I know it's rather rude of me but really, I've dreamed about it so often, I wanted to feast my eyes on it while I could.

'Oh.' Rick exhaled and shifted in his seat. He didn't let go of Luke's erection though. Obviously he didn't want to. I couldn't say I blamed him. I noticed Luke's cheeks were red when I finally looked higher than his crotch but I wasn't sure if that was out of embarrassment or arousal or maybe a bit of both.

'I'm sorry, Claire,' he mumbled, 'I should probably go.'

'Oh, no, you're not getting out of it *that* easily, mate. I did not expect to come home to you guys getting it on.'

'Well, you've always known I was bi.' Rick shrugged. The motion slipped his hand up and down Luke's cock and he bit down on his lip to stop himself moaning.

'Yes, and "was" is the operative word in that sentence. I thought you told me I was all you needed. How you barely even thought of boys any more?'

I was too aroused to be properly angry but I wasn't willing to let go without a fight. It might be a hot bloke he's messing around with but it's still a breach of trust.

'I know and it's true, mostly. But Luke is different and we only ever wank each other off. I don't let him fuck me.'

I would never have guessed that my dominant boyfriend was a bottom. A world of possibilities opened up in my mind as I thought of Luke fucking the shit out of Rick's fine arse or even me doing it. I've always fancied trying a strap-on but it hasn't been a subject I've broached with him.

'Claire, I do love you and I do want to be with you but every now and then I just get this urge for cock,' Rick continued. He'd obviously taken my silence as anger, not a personal fantasy break. 'I can't help it and Luke is my mate and we'll always be mates, just mates.'

'Just mates who play with each other's dicks,' I added

and before Rick could interrupt I continued, 'It's not the need for dick that's worrying me, babe. It's the fact you've kept it from me. I know you're bi. I've listened to your fantasies, remember? Hell, I've even come up with a few of them myself. The problem is that you chose to keep it to yourself. That hurts me.'

'That's my fault.' Luke spoke up. 'Ricky's always wanted to tell you but I've been afraid of you finding out and telling your mates and then maybe the word would get back to my Sophie and she'd kill me.'

I'd forgotten all about Luke's bit of stuff. I'd never met her but heard plenty about her perfect princess ways.

'She doesn't know you're bi?'

'I didn't know until a few months ago,' he said with a shrug.

'Oh.' Now I realise at this point I should have yelled, screamed, stormed out and had a hissy fit. My trust had been misused and I'd been lied to. However, that wasn't the part of the story I chose to focus on. I was too busy thinking about having two very hot bi guys in the room at my beck and call. Maybe I could get to live out one of my favourite fantasies. Well, I had to try and the drinks I'd had at the pub gave me the confidence to go for it.

'Right, well, here's how I see it. You boys are enjoying yourselves and you're doing no one any harm. Rick, we'll have to talk about some trust issues but right now I've had a few and I'm feeling horny. So I'm going to cut right to the chase. If you let me join in with you guys I'll not say a word to my mates about it. What do you think? Go on, talk amongst yourselves.' I waved my hands about. 'I'll take off my coat and shoes and get myself sorted while you decide.'

I tried hard not to listen to their conversation as I took off my coat and hung it up in the hall. I slipped out of my shoes, meaning to do it slowly but really very eager to hear their decision.

'So?' I said as I walked back into the living room. Rick had let go of Luke's dick but it still hung outside his trousers. It was a little limper but I was sure I could fix that in a jiffy.

'We accept,' the guys replied in unison.

'Good,' I said, grinning. 'I was hoping you'd say that. Now continue from where you were. I want to see what you were doing.'

As my boyfriend reasserted his grip on Luke's penis I ran the zip down the back of my night-out dress. The black number slinked down over my curves and left me standing in my best underwear.

'Fuck,' Luke moaned, 'look at those tits.'

'I know, mate,' Rick chirped as he fisted Luke's cock. 'I told you she had a fine set, didn't I?'

'Do you boys discuss my boobs often?' I asked as I sauntered across the living room to join them.

'A bit,' Luke admitted. 'I've always admired your cleavage from afar.'

'Well, now you can appreciate it close up.' I knelt on the floor in front of him. 'Go on, you can touch if you want to.'

He tentatively stretched out and Rick nodded his head in encouragement. I could tell from the bulge in his pants that this idea was turning him on too.

'Wow,' Luke gasped as he stroked the tops of my boobs, 'your skin is so soft, Claire.'

'Thanks,' I said with a smile. 'Now have a proper feel.'

I curved my back and stuck out my breasts proudly. I ached to feel his hard hands around my delicate mounds. I reached behind me and popped open my bra. I slipped the silk down my arms and revealed more of my milky white skin to his sight. Both lads moaned and it resonated deep inside me. They devoured me with their gazes and I revelled in it. When Luke finally got up the courage to cup and squeeze one of my boobs I almost exploded with pleasure. His hands were large and warm and a little rough – from his building work, no doubt. They were similar to Rick's yet it was the thrill of those fingers belonging to someone else that really turned me on.

'God, Rick, you're a fucking lucky man. Her tits are huge and warm and soft. Fuck, I could play with them all day.'

'I know,' Rick replied and reached out with his free

hand. 'I love these tits. And if you play with her nipples, oh, man. She goes wild.'

Rick pinched my nipple and I squealed with delight. Luke soon followed his example and I squirmed under their ministrations. It was my fantasy come true – my knickers were already soaked through and they'd only just felt my breasts.

'I want to touch you, now.' It was all getting too much and I really was desperate to feel some cock. 'I'll keep Luke busy while you get your kit off,' I said to Rick. 'You're far too clothed.'

Luke threw his T-shirt off as Rick removed his own. I crawled forward and Luke parted his thighs to let me in, closer to his magnificent erection. I reverently ran a finger up his length then grasped him firmly in my fist. He was a pleasant handful and I squeezed gently as I ran my hand up and down. There was a bubble of pre-come glistening on the tip of his bulbous head. I slipped out my tongue and licked it off without pausing to think. He tasted like good-quality sushi.

'Fuck,' he groaned and grabbed a handful of my brunette curls. 'Ricky, mate, she's even better than you told me.'

'Once tried, never forgotten. That's my Claire.' I glanced to the side and noticed with satisfaction that Rick was naked. A shot of lust ran through me and I licked my lips. My man has a good body, lean and wiry but strong and long in all the right places. 'Suck his knob, love,' he urged me. 'Give him the deluxe treatment.'

I nodded then stretched my neck forward to capture Luke's cock between my lips. Slowly I enveloped him and fed him deeper into my mouth until my lips bumped against my fist. I moved hand and mouth in unison and felt Luke stiffen.

'Holy hell,' he gasped, 'Ricky, mate, no wonder you're always smiling.'

I chuckled around his cock and the air vibration tickled my lips as I continued to enjoy the taste of a new man in my mouth. As I savoured the sea salt and citrus tang I closed my eyes and lost myself in the moment. It's not every day you get to feast on a tasty new cock, and I was determined to enjoy every moment of it. I heard the sound of lips locking and opened my eyes to find Rick and Luke sharing a particularly passionate snog. My cunt clenched as a vision from one of my dirtier fantasies unfolded before me. I'd always wanted to see my Rick with another man. I imagined him kissing another guy to be so hot. I hadn't been wrong. The contrast of Rick's soft smooth cheek against Luke's stubble-covered one had me wondering how it'd feel to be sandwiched between the two of them. I wanted to pull Rick's blond hair, curl its length around my fingers, and to smooth over the dark short cut of Luke's. Push their heads lower and lower until they'd be fighting over licking my snatch.

'Whatcha thinkin'?' Rick whispered when he noticed me staring at them.

'Oh, just wondering what it'd feel like to have your mouths on my body,' I replied, 'since you're both so deliciously different.'

'Let's try it!' they choroused in unison. Rick laughed and continued on his own, 'Hop up on the sofa, love, and we'll show you how it feels.' I scrambled up and the boys pulled apart so I could nestle between them. They started by kissing a cheek each. Rick's kiss was familiar and soft whereas Luke's was harder. I loved the gentle pricking of his stubble against me. But I wouldn't tell Rick that; I always nagged him to keep clean-shaven. I liked him that way.

'Shall we go lower?' Luke cooed in my ear. His breath tickled and made me shiver. I nodded, unable to form words let alone force them from my mouth. If you've never felt the caress of two pairs of lips on your body then you're missing out, truly. We all know how delicious it is to have a lover lavish us with oral attention but it only gets better when you double the number. The subtle differences between Luke's kiss and Rick's were many and I would revisit them in my dreams. The way Luke would nibble on my flesh between kisses, or how Rick sucked with such force on my nipple while Luke's treatment of my breast was gentler but equally arousing.

As their lips sank lower their hands did too. A male

hand on either side slipped down between my thighs. Each hand pulled a leg back, spreading me wide open. The cool air caressed my wet lips and made me long for a relieving touch down there. My clit was hard and aching and needed attention.

'Can I touch her pussy, Ricky?' Luke gasped as he looked down my body. I felt a zing of strange arousal as I realised he was asking for permission to play with me like I was just a possession. It riled me up but not in the way you might think. I loved being the object of their desires.

'Sure, mate, sure. She's gagging for it. Can you see how wet she is?'

He ran a long hard finger along my thigh and dragged my moisture with it. My cheeks flared with heat. I don't know if it was embarrassment or lust or more likely a mixture of both, but I felt deliciously sexual and anxious for more. I wanted Luke to discover just how much I wanted him – no, how much I wanted *them* – to fuck me.

'So wet,' he whispered as his fingers crawled up towards my slit. 'Her thighs are soaked.'

'Told you she was a slut.'

I opened my mouth to protest but Rick pressed his finger to my lips. The finger that tasted of me. 'Shush, love. You know it's true.'

He was right. I was a slut, his slut. Let's face it, good girls don't desire two men at the same time.

I thought no more as Luke's fingers moved up and down my slit and hit my clit. I bumped up my hips and moaned. Luke realised what I liked and focused on my hard nub. It's so difficult to explain how different it felt to have his fingers pressing me there. The movement was similar to Rick's but the pressure was lighter and the finger more ridged and rough. I was so turned on I couldn't believe I could feel any more, but then Rick used his fingers to fuck me and I went to a whole new level of arousal.

'Watch her,' Rick whispered between kisses on my neck, 'watch her as she comes. It's the most beautiful thing on fucking earth.'

I groaned and the boys continued to finger-fuck me and manipulate my clit until I stiffened and yelled as the ecstasy ripped through my body. I felt worshipped and adored and I loved Rick all the more for his pride in me. I was thrilled by how he wanted to share me, to show me off.

'She tastes so good.' Luke licked his fingers eagerly.

'It's better from the source,' Rick said with a wink.

'Really? Won't she be too sensitive?'

'Fuck, no. She can go for bloody hours. Just be gentle at first, let her clit recover a bit.'

I was far too engrossed in the tingling sensations suffusing my body to join in the conversation. Rick was right. I could go for hours sometimes. I knew I was lucky to have multiple orgasms so easily.

Luke got down off the sofa and onto the floor between my knees. He sat and looked at me for a moment. I wanted to squirm, to cover my stomach. It was a silly reaction and Luke said as much.

'You're beautiful, Claire. I'm taking in the details. Don't cover up, not a single inch. You're perfect.'

I felt Rick nod against my breast. I was the luckiest woman in the world. I had two men who thought I was gorgeous. Fuck society, I decided. I would revel in my curves just as they did.

The first tentative lick Luke gave made me shudder. He squirmed his tongue between my lips and lapped up my juices.

'You like that, don't you?' Rick whispered against my ear, his arm across my body, his fingers tweaking my nipple.

'Yes,' I replied with a throaty moan.

'You like my best mate's tongue in your cunt, don't you? You want his cock in there too, don't you?'

'Yes,' I gasped again.

'You're going to get it, my slut, and more, because I'm going to fuck your arse at the same time. Yeah, you're going to be fucked by us both.'

'Oh, fuck, yes.' I bucked up against Luke's face, his eager lapping driving me wild.

'Mate, she's desperate for your cock,' Rick told Luke. 'Grab a condom out of the fruit bowl, just under the bananas.'

I giggled nervously. I didn't like sex toys, didn't need them. I preferred something more natural when I couldn't get the real thing. Not that that was a problem now. I had two eager dicks willing to please me.

'Stand up.' Rick pulled me up as Luke crawled, then stood up and walked over to the table to get the condoms.

Rick wrapped his arms around me and kissed me passionately. His hand dropped to my arse and slapped me. I jumped with surprise then melted into his arms with liquid groans as he continued to spank me.

'Naughty girl,' he hissed when our lips parted. 'My gorgeous, naughty girl.'

'Don't worry, Lukey boy,' Rick explained, 'she fucking loves a spanking. Come on, lie down on the sofa, mate. I'm just keeping her warm for you.'

'God, you're so lucky, Rick. Sophie would freak out if I tried to spank her.'

'Luckiest man alive, I am. Now you get to find out exactly why.' Rick turned me towards the couch and walked away. I smiled at Luke, who was lying back on the sofa. He'd already sheathed his erection ready for me.

'You must be desperate to come by now,' I said as I straddled him, 'you've been waiting for ages.'

'Yes,' he hissed as I positioned myself at the top of his cock and pushed down. 'I really want to fucking come, Claire. I want to come inside you.'

I moved slowly up and down on his hardness, getting

used to his dimensions. He was thicker than Rick but not as long and it took me a moment to get the rhythm and the depth of my movements just right.

'Oh, fuck, Claire. I love seeing his cock in you.' I felt Rick pull open my buttocks. I gasped at the eroticism of it all. My boyfriend could now see every intimate detail of his friend's cock fucking me.

'Now then, my turn,' he muttered. I heard the plastic click of a bottle opening and felt a cold wet finger at my arsehole.

'Fuck,' I gasped and tried to relax. I knew it would be easier if I let him push into me without tensing up.

'Does it hurt?' Luke asked me as I stilled, his dick lodged inside me.

'Not really,' I replied and kissed him. 'It just feels strange. I have to relax, let him get his fingers into me.'

'How does it feel?' Luke whispered. 'I really want to know.'

As Rick slipped fingers into me, opening me up, readying me for his cock, I tried to explain the sensation.

'It's just a big pressure at first, you feel like you might break apart, but then, as the rhythm builds and you relax, it feels good. It's different to the sensations I get when my pussy is fingered or fucked. It's a rawer, deeper, more visceral arousal. I feel it like lightning bolts shooting through me. It's so intense it's almost too much but not quite enough ... I don't know if I'm describing this well.'

'No, you are,' he replied, nuzzling my neck. 'I really can't wait to have my arse fucked or to fuck an arse. I've never done either before.'

'Fuck,' I moaned, 'I wish I could see that.'

'Mmm, well, maybe you could be the one fucking me?' he replied.

'Fuck, yes, that'd be so hot,' Rick moaned. 'Then Luke could fuck your arse, darling, and I could watch.'

He gasped. I knew he'd love that. From the look on Luke's face, he'd enjoy it too.

'Now hold still, my pet. I'm going to fuck your arse now. Luke, hold her open for me, mate, please.'

Luke reached round me and pulled apart my buttocks with his strong fingers. I was tingling all over. I couldn't wait to feel my lover's cock inside me too. I had felt full with his fingers in there against Luke's dick – how would I cope with two dicks in me? I didn't know but I was incredibly eager to find out. Rick was right. I was a total slut and I loved it. I felt alive and free and really fucking horny.

Rick pushed his foot down between the sofa back and my knee, then his covered cock slipped down between my buttocks. 'All right doll, relax, I'm going to push into you now.'

Rick always made sure I was prepared. I loved him for how much he cared about my comfort.

'Oh, fuck, Luke, he's pushing into me,' I moaned.

'Yeah, I can feel it. I can feel the tip of him inside you.'

'I feel so full, jeez, and he's only got the head in.'

'OK, darling, that was the hard part,' Rick purred. He stroked my back. 'Just relax and let us fuck you.'

'Yes,' I yelled, 'oh, yes, fuck me.'

I was so wet and ready and needy. Rick pushed into me and I felt like I would explode but not in a bad way. The lads worked out a rhythm between them. Rick did most of the work with Luke pulling back and pushing in as he obviously came closer and closer to coming. I held on and rode the orgasms that rolled through my body. Every movement sent more ecstasy through my blood. I felt light-headed with lust and I didn't want it to end but I could tell from the grunts and groans of the guys that they were close.

Luke emptied into me first. His body shook and he dug his nails into my hips as he stilled. His head was thrown back, his mouth open wide in a silent scream. He relaxed back with a moan that sent tingles through my body.

'Gonna come,' Rick panted, 'oh, fuck, gonna come.'

'Yes, baby, that's it,' I cooed, focusing on his pleasure, wanting him to feel as good as I had felt. 'Fuck my arse, Rick, come for me.'

His fingers bit into my shoulders as he pushed deep into my back passage. I felt his cock throb and heard his roar of satisfaction. I didn't want to think what the neighbours might think was going on in here.

We slowly untangled limbs and shifted around on the sofa. I was between the two lads, whose bodies were sheened with sweat just like mine. We all panted in unison, all replete from our actions.

'What are you thinking?' Rick asked as the silence dragged on.

'Oh, I was just thinking of all the fantasies I could make come true with you two.'

'Like what?' Luke enquired.

'OK, well, I'd love to see you sucking his dick for a start. I'd love to have both of you going down on me at the same time. I want to feel Rick's cock in my cunt as I suck your cock and drink down your come. I want to fuck your arse. I want to watch you fuck Rick and vice versa and –'

'Whoa there, honey.' Rick stuck his hand in front of him, the universal signal for 'stop'. I wondered if I'd gone too far. 'Let us catch our breath first, please.'

Luke laughed and I joined in, their manly chuckles highlighted by my sweeter giggles.

'All right, I'll give you five minutes.' I nodded solemnly.

'Good, that's just long enough for us to get on the net and order you a strap-on,' Rick replied with a wink.

Luke's eyes widened, his cheeks flushed red. 'Oh, you remembered I said that, then.'

'Too right, mate,' Rick answered, 'I can't wait to see my missus fucking you.'

'She'll have to break the damn thing in first, though. She'll have to fuck you first, Ricky lad.' Luke winked at me and I rolled my eyes. This could go on for quite a while.

'No, no, you go first, son, I insist.'

The lads continued their banter as they stood and wandered off to the computer in the back room.

'Well, that decides it,' I mumbled to myself, 'in future I'm going to spend more nights in with the boys.'

There's a Hole
Giselle Renarde

He gazed up at her while she looked down on him.

It was the same thing every lunch hour: all the ladies working in nearby office buildings descended from their glass towers to watch the workers heave and haul in the construction pit. Good old Donna liked to brag that those women came to ogle her beefy body, but Lennox doubted many of them were lesbians.

'Here they are!' Donna cheered, pointing up at the women staring down at them through the tall chain-link fence. 'Every day like clockwork they come to check me out.'

Lennox shook his head. 'You're one cocky dyke, you know that?'

'Hey, Ox, think I should take off my shirt?' she teased. 'Whip it around over my head, get the ladies riled up?'

He tried to focus on the job, but until their foreman

143

got back from some meeting they didn't have much to do. Lennox hated standing around. He felt guilty knowing the company was shelling out good money while he spent half the day waiting in a hole.

'Maybe we should cut some new planks,' he said to Donna.

'I say we climb up and say hello to those fawning ladies.' Donna hopped up on the rungs amidst a tower of scaffolding and began the arduous ascent.

When most people thought about high-rise construction, they pictured steel girders soaring to the sun. They'd get to that point with this building, but they weren't there yet. Every big building started out as a big hole. Just like trees, buildings needed deep roots. This hole descended halfway to hell.

'Fine,' Donna shouted from the ladder. 'Guess if you're not coming up I get these ladies all to myself.' Which would have been fine, until she added, 'Even the one in the blue polka-dot dress!'

How the hell did she know? Had Lennox really been so obvious?

'OK, I'll come.' No way he'd let Donna get at that girl. Of that entire mass of office workers, she was the only one he was sweet on. There was something special about her: small and subtle, refined without being fussy, long brown hair blowing in the breeze.

Not that he'd ever said a word to the woman. In

fact, every time their gazes met, he quickly looked away. Something in the prettiness of her smile made him inexplicably bashful.

Lennox resented being cast as a male chauvinist pig just because he worked in construction. He wasn't like that, not at all. Lennox wouldn't feel comfortable on a jobsite where catcalling and wolf-whistling were common practice, not in a million years. Hell, he might be strong as an ox, but women made him nervous. He didn't like it when the office workers congregated at street level to watch his muscles writhe and strain. Their eyes struck his skin like needles, lustful but nevertheless castigating.

Actually, the trouble wasn't their eyes but their concept of who he was: just another dumb guy, too stupid for a real job, toiling away in a big hole, stuck for life. That was what they thought of him, wasn't it? Good enough for a hot fuck, but lacking sufficient brain power to carry on an intelligent conversation.

'Tough climb,' Donna called, leading the vertical way.

'Sure is.' Lennox's muscles strained as he heaved his body up rung by rung, feeling the sun beating down on his back, sweat beading and slipping down his spine.

When he reached the top, Donna was already showing off for the ladies, who were polite enough, saying, 'It's encouraging, seeing women on jobsites. Must be hard work.'

'Yup,' Donna shot back. 'You gotta be good and strong to tackle a job like this.'

145

The crowd turned its attention to Lennox as he pulled himself out of the pit and onto the wooden platform. It was sturdy enough and there was a railing, but anyone who took that plunge would never again see the light of day. The drop was a long one, and the first concrete layer of foundation had already set.

'What are you building?' asked a woman with a purple suit jacket tossed over one arm. 'Is it offices or more condos?'

Lennox felt limp with all those eyes on him, and he was glad when Donna answered, 'A hotel! Nice fancy-ass place, I hear.'

While Donna showed off her knowledge of the project, Lennox took the opportunity to steal a glance at the girl who made his heart thunder. Oh shit, she was staring at him too! He'd never seen anyone so naturally pretty. Everything about her seemed so clean and fresh, like white linen, like daisies. She was everything he wasn't, in his dirty, sun-soaked skin. She was everything he craved.

He watched her unabashedly bite her sandwich: lettuce and tomatoes and cheese on a triangular bun. No nail polish. Up close, she didn't seem to have any make-up on at all. Lennox liked that. He wished this big crowd and Donna and the tall fence would all disappear, and they could be alone together, just Lennox and the girl in the polka-dot dress.

When she smiled at him and waved, still chewing her

sandwich, Lennox nearly lost his cool. He took a step back, fumbled against the railing, and Donna cried, 'Ox! Watch it or you'll break your neck.'

He felt stupid, clumsy and embarrassed, but the girl in the polka-dot dress smiled gently. It was like they had their own language, and they spoke it in silence. They understood each other without words.

Donna was still showing off for the group, but he couldn't draw his attention away from that beautiful girl on the other side of the fence. He loved the way the summer breeze played with her dress, the hem teasing her knees, dancing in the wind. Wisps of light-brown hair followed suit.

Lennox wondered if she could see the poetry in his heart.

'Donna! Ox! What the hell are you doing at ground level?' The foreman was back on the scene, chasing them into the pit.

Just as Lennox set foot on the ladder, he heard a wispy voice beyond the fence. 'Ox?'

It was the girl in the blue polka-dot dress! He met her gaze and smiled.

'That's your name, right?' she asked. 'Ox?'

'Lennox,' he told her. They were actually talking! This was like a dream. 'But you can call me Lenny or Len, or Lennox or Ox. Call me whatever you want.'

'I'm Fern,' she said.

'You look like a fern,' he replied, so quickly he almost swallowed his tongue. 'Not that you're green or anything, just ... you look like you could live in a forest.'

He pictured her asleep on a bed of ferns under a leafy canopy, her naked skin glistening with dew. His cock pounded the interior of his jeans as he imagined kissing every inch of her body, then taking her in that forest of dreams, filling her wetness with steel heat, pumping, thrusting his hips, driving his body into hers while she mewled like a sleepy kitten.

'Into the pit, Ox!' the boss hollered.

Lennox hated getting in trouble, but he couldn't look away from lovely Fern.

'What time do you get off?' she asked quickly.

The words made him swallow hard. He was sweating again, and it wasn't the sun's rays this time. 'Four-thirty,' he said.

'I'm not done until five,' she told him through the fence. 'I'll meet you here after work, OK?'

'Yes,' Lennox managed as his boss stomped the boards, shooing him into the hole.

All afternoon, he was lost in a haze of Fern fantasies. She was the wood nymph, frolicking naked in the forest, friend to birds and the animals. Together they made love up against trees and down in the soft groundcover. He took her every way possible, enjoying the sweet taste of her centre and then watching as she took him in her

148

pretty little mouth and sucked. He imagined flipping her to her hands and knees in the gentle undergrowth and infiltrating her wet heat from behind, watching her grasp at green things while he moved deep inside of her, so deep they would always be connected. And when he filled her with his essence, she replied in kind, soaking him with the juice of her arousal.

Emotion in motion. That's what Lennox wanted.

'Quittin' time, Ox!' Donna slapped him on the shoulder and led the way towards the ladder.

If only he had time to shower and shave, but the commute would take too long. He felt a bit embarrassed that they'd have to meet like this, his body still slick with the day's sweat, his hair dusty, clothing caked with concrete and dirt. He cleaned up nice, and he wanted to show her, but it would have to be another day. In this state, no good restaurant would have him, and Fern was the sort of girl who deserved the best.

Under the shade of a nearby maple, Lennox pulled the well-worn copy of *Animal Farm* from his lunchbox. He tried to focus on the words, but in his mind's eye all he could see was Fern approaching like a mirage, her polka-dot dress fluttering in the breeze. She'd come to him and, without words, take the book from his hand, toss it away and straddle his big body while she leaned in to plant a luscious kiss on his lips.

He would open up for her, and she for him, and they

to each other. Her hands would touch his neck, soft as a kitten's paws, and trace a brave path down his chest. Feeling emboldened by her desire, Lennox would grab her thighs, pull her dress up over the curve of her behind, knead those sweet white mounds of flesh. Her skin would be the creamiest he'd even encountered. Her mouth would taste like cucumber and spearmint, like water, like relief.

As they kissed, she would pry open his belt, her little fingers working away until the aromatic leather gave way to her want.

'Yesss,' Lennox would hiss, mimicking the sound of his zipper as she pulled it down, snapped open the button and stretched his fly to form an impressive V.

And then she'd seek out his cock, find it hard and expose it to the afternoon air. She'd wrap her little fist around his thick shaft and pump his straining meat, having no idea of the ache she'd caused him for so many days. His cock had strained for her, though he'd begged it to settle down. She had no idea of the sweet throb she'd sparked in him.

'Lennox?'

He looked up and there she was, little white purse slung over her shoulder, polka-dot dress dancing in the wind.

'Fern!'

She giggled softly and shaded her mouth with perfect fingers. 'Why so surprised?'

Everything he might have said sounded silly in his

head, so he settled on, 'I'm glad you're here.'

She stared at him, which would have made him nervous if she'd been anyone else. And then she said, 'Can we go down in the hole?'

The hole? 'Why would you want to go there? It's dirty.'

Fern cocked her head. Her hair cascaded over her shoulder like a glistening waterfall. 'Maybe *I'm* dirty.'

Lennox replayed those words in his mind: *maybe I'm dirty, maybe I'm dirty, maybe I'm dirty.* Was she joking, or was this for real? It was like a dream.

'Everything's locked up, hard hats and all that,' Lennox stammered. 'And those shoes won't stand up to a work site.'

Fern glanced at her shoes, which were the flat kind, no heels. They sort of looked like ballet slippers, except they were shiny and blue. 'I'll be OK. I'll stay close to you, and you'll make sure nothing bad happens.'

A surge of power blasted through his body, pounding in his gut before stiffening his already solid cock. His erection throbbed against his jeans, like a desperate lover hammering at his dear one's door, screaming, 'Let me in! I want inside!'

'It isn't safe,' Lennox said, though he knew he was faltering. When he looked into those greeny-brown eyes, he couldn't say no. 'OK, but stick close by.'

'Right up against you,' she agreed as he unhinged the gate, moved the sandbags away and swung it open.

When Fern wrapped a slender arm around him, he felt crazy with the swell of dazed lust.

'I want to go down,' Fern pleaded, leading him to the scaffolding. 'You first.'

He couldn't argue with her.

He climbed down a few rungs, then watched her turn around and set one little blue slipper on the gritty, rusting metal. The breeze caught her dress as she descended, and Lennox tried to look away, but he wasn't fast enough. He caught a glimpse and then he couldn't get it out of his mind: no panties! Fern wasn't wearing anything at all underneath her dress!

'Go down,' she instructed, but Lennox just gripped the metal rungs. His arms were shaking, all muscles in spasm, cock pounding against his jeans, begging for release.

Fern settled in close to his body, as close as possible without getting inside his clothes. When he caught the lily-fresh scent of her skin, Lennox felt so dizzied he was sure he'd fall to his death. Her bottom, which he knew was bare under that blue dress, set into the saddle of his hips, pressing against his swollen cock, and he couldn't help himself – he groaned.

Fern giggled before Lennox could feel too embarrassed, and repeated, 'Go down.'

This time he did, making sure Fern's slender body stayed close to his, curled within his protective strength like a joey in a kangaroo's pouch. But Fern kept laughing, and when they were about three storeys from the foundation, he finally asked, 'What's so funny?'

He continued his descent, but Fern halted and slowly turned around. Gripping the bars above her head, she spread her legs until she was straddling the scaffolding. Lennox's heart raced, not only because he could see right up her skirt, but because he was afraid she might jump.

Then she said, 'Go down … on me,' and all at once he felt numb.

This was crazy, but her naked flesh called to him. He tried to resist the siren's song, but its pull was overwhelming. He climbed up a few rungs and let his head bob beneath Fern's fluttering dress. It was dark under there, but he followed the tangy sweet scent to find heat between her legs. As his eyes adjusted, he swiftly realised Fern's pussy was wholly shaven, and his legs began to shake.

Holding the rung behind her back, Lennox closed in on her sizzling pussy and ran his lips across the smoothness of her mound. He could hear her gasping and wished he could see her face, but he imagined her blissful expression as he ran his tongue up her soft folds. Was she ever wet! She must have been thinking about this all afternoon, planning it in her head as she sat at her desk, doing whatever it was she did for a living. He didn't even know!

This really wasn't like him, but right now it didn't matter. All that mattered was Fern's desire, Fern's pleasure. Licking her wet folds under the darkness of her dress, he zeroed in on her clit. It wasn't hard to find – it stuck out like a button waiting to be pushed. With his tongue he tickled her slippery clit, flicking up and down with the tip, teasing her. When she moaned loud enough for him to hear, he ran circles around the engorged bud, slow and sensual, though he could hardly bear the pace.

'Suck it!' she cried.

God, she was loud. Suddenly Lennox worried about his job. What if someone noticed them down here and told his boss? He'd get fired for sure.

'Suck my clit!' Fern insisted, even louder this time. 'Suck it in your big strong fucking macho mouth!'

Lennox was shocked by her language, but even his shock couldn't dampen his arousal. Splaying her pussy with his mouth, he latched on and encircled her inner lips. No, that wasn't good enough. He opened his mouth wider, spreading over as much of her mound as he could handle. His tongue sought the source of her wetness and infiltrated her like a serpent, sneaky but virile.

'Holy fuck!' Fern shouted. She pushed his head against her crotch, which meant she must have let go of the rung with one hand, and that worried Lennox immensely, though not enough to make him stop.

'I don't know what you're doing down there, but it's fucking incredible!' Fern cried as she bucked her crotch against his face.

He worried that she'd lose her foothold on the scaffolding and slip, sending them both crashing down. All Lennox could do was cling to her, grasping the bar behind her back, holding her so tight she wouldn't be able to fall. As he gripped her slim body, his need to bring her bliss came to a head, and he pulled his tongue from her pussy, slathering her clit with her own sweet juices. God, he loved the taste of her: musky but mild, like nothing else that had ever been on his tongue.

Lennox licked her pussy hot and fast, licked her entire slit from the base of her hole to the arch of her clit. He pressed his tongue flat against her wet flesh and shook his head madly in all directions.

Bucking against his face, Fern cried out what might have been words, but he couldn't hear very well through her dress. His face was dripping with her juices. With every lick, more nectar slid down his chin and dripped like melted fire against his chest. He felt wet everywhere, like she was sliding off of him, and that made him worry, so he held her tighter.

'I'm gonna come so fucking hard!' Fern cried out, holding his head between her legs – using both hands? Had she really let go of the rung? Was he bearing all her weight? 'Lenny, baby, suck my clit!'

He did, and she exploded, soaking his face with sweet pussy juice. It ran down his cheeks and chin while she cursed a blue streak. Her hips rattled, her pelvis slammed his face and he felt the quiver of her muscles as he waited out the storm. She was the ocean waves and he was the beach. Her tides crashed against him, one and then another, and another, her orgasms exploding against his tongue.

Lost in a dream, he let her find her bearings before ducking out of her dress. He must look messy as hell, his face bathed in her juices. She shot him a bashful smile before turning around. As they climbed into the construction pit, Lennox's cock ached for release, sending bolts of genuine pain through his balls every time he moved.

They stood together at the base of the scaffolding, close but not close enough. He needed to be inside of her. Her pussy was right there, beneath just a single layer of fabric. It was pulpy and wet. Juice was probably coursing down her thighs as she gazed around the jobsite.

Shielding her eyes from the sun, Fern pointed at the metal behemoth in the centre of the hole. 'Can we go up in the crane?'

'Are you kidding? It's a good ten-storey drop from the top of that thing, and I don't have keys to the booth.'

When she didn't respond, he felt guilty for offering such a flip response, but before long she'd wandered to the huge pile of sand pushed up against one corner of the site.

'It's like the beach,' she said, climbing the hill. 'We can sunbathe.'

Lennox and his aching cock and his strained balls

followed her. In that polka-dot dress she belonged to another time and place, and Lennox had to ask himself if she was really there at all. Maybe she was a figment of his imagination. Maybe he'd fallen and taken a blow to the head. Could be that he was in hospital right now, and Fern was just a coma fantasy.

Her voice filled his head like gauze, floating between his ears, and he realised she was asking him questions – about himself, about the book he'd been reading. His lust overwhelmed his senses, but he felt constrained. It would be ungentlemanly to take her in this pile of sand. So he answered her questions, pleased to have someone in his life who was so interested in him.

When twilight fell, Fern leaped up and shot across the jobsite. She headed for the crane and climbed the ladder in the middle of its central structure. 'Come with me, Lennox!'

'Get down from there,' he replied, racing after her, wanting to keep her safe. His erection was now so huge and hefty it felt like a third leg, and every time it rubbed against the ladder's rungs he felt like he was going to burst. 'Please, Fern, this is very dangerous.'

She'd nearly reached the top when her shoe slipped off her foot. It narrowly missed hitting Lennox in the face, and his heart beat wildly. She giggled and said a quick 'sorry', but he was so afraid for her, so afraid she'd fall. Still, it was hard to keep from looking up her dress.

Huffing, Lennox arrived at the top of the crane tower and pulled himself onto the railed-in platform outside the locked cab. 'Fern! Get down!'

She was perched on the railing, both feet curled around the metal posts, gazing at the emerging stars. 'Beautiful up here.'

'Please.' He stepped close to her and wrapped his arms around her lean body. 'It's a ten-storey drop. If you fell …'

'I already have,' she whispered in his ear, and he started to panic before realising that was a metaphor.

Before he knew it, her soft lips were on his, her tongue sweeping into his mouth, mingling hotly with his. He tensed, then melted into her, kissing her hard, running his big hands through her hair. A feeling of possession came over him, and he trapped her in his arms. He would never let her fall, never. She was his completely.

She was sliding down his body now, pressing her warm front against his throbbing cock. Did she realise how he ached for her?

When her feet met the metal platform, Fern turned around, pushed her beautiful bottom against his crotch and stroked him like that. 'I want you to fuck me up here,' she said.

How could he possibly refuse?

Lennox fumbled with his belt, his fly, hoping it was too dark for anyone to see, but knowing the city lights were probably illuminating them from below. Normally he wasn't the type to take off his pants for the entire population, but Fern's soft body broke down his resistance.

She pulled up her skirt with one hand, gripping the metal bar in front of her with the other. Though his head had been under her skirt not long before, the sight of her exposed bum made his cock jump, begging for it.

Still, he asked, 'Are you sure?'

'Yes!' she hissed. 'Fuck me into the middle of next week!'

He'd waited too long as it was, and his cock was so hard it hurt. Fern's slit was every bit as wet as it had been when he'd eaten her. He rubbed his cockhead up and down her white-hot flesh, searching for the place where it would give access, like a secret panel.

'Get inside,' Fern demanded, and he followed her order gladly, shoving himself forward, letting his cock find its way in the dark.

He soared inside the pink of her, feeling her pussy hug him, milk his length while he hammered forward. Hopefully he wasn't hurting her, because he didn't think he could stop. Her pussy was so tight, so pulpy and blazing that he just couldn't quit.

'Fuck me!' Fern growled, bucking her butt into the saddle of his hips. The pressure drove him wild, bringing him to the brink. Watching didn't help. Lennox closed his eyes, but all he could see was his cock streaming into Fern's cunt, both slathered in juice, her asshole winking conspiratorially.

'Oh God!' Lennox traced his hands up her front and squeezed her little tits, and she pulled down the top of her dress to give him better access.

Her flesh was hot, her nipples erect, and he pinched them, twisted, feeling her pussy clamp down on his dick. 'Fuck, that's good!' Fern gasped. 'Keep playing with my tits, big boy.'

Her voice rose higher in pitch the harder he pinched her, the harder he pummelled her with his cock. He couldn't hold out much longer. His cock throbbed like a fist inside Fern's tight pussy, his balls surging to the apex of his thighs, legs shaking, trembling.

Lennox launched inside Fern, opening his eyes to take in the dizzying sight of their bodies locked together. Beyond them, a ten-storey drop. He gripped her tighter, squeezing her breasts. She gasped, gripping the railing, shoving her ass against his pelvis. 'Yes! Fill me, Lennox.'

His name on her tongue took him over the edge, and as his come shot into her he felt like he was falling, going right over the edge and tumbling into oblivion.

'Yes,' he echoed, breathing in the light scent of her hair, worshipping her from behind. The spasms in his thighs and balls continued as she bucked against him, grunting and cursing.

He felt dizzy, too weak to stand, and brought her down with him till they were sitting on the platform. He hugged Fern tight. His cock was, miraculously, still inside of her, and it could stay there for ever as far as he was concerned.

They breathed together, panting at first, then gasping and sighing, then laughing. Petting her beautiful hair, Lennox asked, 'What happened here tonight?'

She looked up into the starlit sky, and he followed her gaze, hugging her tighter. 'Love,' Fern replied, like it was just that simple. 'Tonight we fell in love.'

As illogical as it seemed, seeing as they hadn't even spoken until this afternoon, Lennox knew Fern was right. He felt the danger of her in his heart and throbbing in his cock, which was already firming up for another round. In the fragrance of her hair, Lennox could sense the future stretching out in front of them. From all the way up here, on the platform of this crane jutting into the night sky, he could see it all.

Road Show
Heather Towne

Christopher Dent hopped off the freight train just short of the Mississippi border. He knew the railroad bulls took a real hard attitude to free-riders in the Magnolia State; that the law backed them up with the toughest vagrancy raps in the country. He'd done a couple of stretches in county jails before, and he didn't want to do any more if he could avoid it.

Besides, Christopher was sick of riding the rails, being everybody's punk up and down the line. He was nineteen, slim and tanned and boyish, with bright-blue eyes and straw-blond hair, a hot property amongst the hobos; a road punk to fight over, then fondle and fuck. It wasn't getting Christopher anything more than a few minutes of pleasure, his travels going nowhere fast. 'Bos aren't loaded with dough by nature, and Christopher wanted his slice of the pie, Depression or no Depression.

162

So, when he spotted the travelling circus setting up shop on the right side of the line, on the outskirts of some hick Tennessee town, he made a beeline. Circusing was hard work for the labourers and roustabouts, but the freaks and carnival barkers made a pretty good living without breaking their backs. Enough, at least, to set them up for the winter.

It was a ten-car show, made up of railroad coaches and vans and flat-decks. There were animal acts, acrobats, freak shows, midway games, gambling wheels and even a cooch show. Christopher found the bossman, Bull Suggs, yelling his lungs out at the straining, sweating stiffs rigging the big top.

'I'm looking for a job, Mr Suggs,' he piped, clutching his cap in his little hands and shuffling his little feet in the dirt, batting his long blond eyelashes.

Suggs was well over six feet, two hundred pounds, a big brick-red-complexioned man with fiery red hair. He was wearing a checked suit almost as loud and obnoxious as his voice, a long green cigar plugged into the corner of his surprisingly sensual mouth. He growled, 'We're full up, 'bo. Take it on the lam.'

Christopher pushed a trembling hand through his hair as big sparkling tears suddenly welled up in his eyes and rolled down his baby cheeks. 'I'll – I'll do anything you ask, Mr Suggs,' he blubbered. Then bit into his plush red lower lip with his small bright-white teeth.

Suggs blasted more profanity at the work crew, then uncorked the stogie from his kisser and gave Christopher the once-over. His hard brown eyes lingered on the young man's slim body and pretty face, the greasy gears in his dirty mind grinding. 'Well ... mebbe I can use you, at that. What'd you say your name was?'

'Christopher Dent, sir.'

Suggs wound his thick red tongue around the sodden end of his cigar, contemplating some more. Then he made up his mind. 'OK ... Chrissie. Follow me.'

He led Christopher into his office aboard the first coach of the sidetracked train of cars. It was packed tighter than a hobo's bindle, papers and parts and costumes and posters strewn all over the place. Suggs dug his meaty paws into a steamer trunk and pulled out a long blonde wig and a short black dress. 'One of the girls just pulled outta the cooch show. Some yokel knocked her up and she hitched her wagon to the rube.' He threw the dress and wig at Christopher. 'Think you can pull it off?'

The young man caught the beauty items and stared at them, then up at the bossman. 'You mean ...'

Suggs nodded, serious as shooting.

He helped Christopher off with his dusty road rags, until the blond was totally naked. Then he roamed his big brawny hands over the smooth bronze flesh of Christopher's narrow shoulders, down the supple curve of the young man's back, onto the taut rounded humps of Christopher's buttocks.

Christopher's puffy tan nipples stiffened and swelled at the hot heavy touch of the big man, in the close confines of the car. His cock did the same, rising up from his blond-fuzzed loins to sniff at the stuffy air, lengthening and thickening and pointing. Suggs wrapped a hand around the swelling appendage and tugged on it.

'You look just like a young gal,' he breathed in Christopher's ear, as the pair of them stared at the nude, lewd reflection in the cracked tilt-mirror mounted in the corner. ''Cept for one obvious exception.' Suggs leered and squeezed Christopher's fully erect, pulsating penis.

Christopher leaned back against the man, feeling the firm, heated grip on his engorged cock all through his body, basking in the shimmering warmth.

Until Suggs suddenly let out a bellow, almost shattering Christopher's eardrum. An old hag answered the raucous call, slipping in from a neighbouring berth.

'This here's the Scarecrow,' Suggs informed the startled 'bo. 'She'll doll you up good.'

'Scarecrow' was right, Christopher thought. The woman was wizened and crooked like she'd had the stuffing knocked out of her, her weathered face and body left out in the elements too long.

Suggs explained his idea to the hag, and she let out a cackle of agreement, then went to work.

The Scarecrow hung a bra around Christopher's hairless chest, added some cotton stuffing, then slid a pair of silk panties up the young man's slender legs and over his deflating cock. She helped him on with a pair of silk stockings, then the dress, then a pair of three-inch black heels. She broke out a make-up kit and powdered Christopher's face, painted him with eye-shadow and lipstick, perfumed the rest of his body.

'We'll shave every inch of you later,' she crowed, 'just to be sure.'

She and Suggs admired their handiwork in the mirror while Christopher blushed. He really *did* look like a woman, a young, desirable woman.

Suggs shoved the Scarecrow out the door, snarling, 'Leave us alone a minute, will ya.'

He crowded up behind Christopher again and put his hands back on the young man's shoulders, glaring at the reflection in the mirror, breathing hard against Christopher's slender neck. 'You'll drive the rubes nuts, that's for sure, Chrissie,' he rumbled, pressing his hard cock in between Christopher's buttocks.

Suggs kissed Christopher's neck, soft and wet, then hard and sharp. He bit into the blond's neck while one of his hands curved around onto the young man's chest, cupped and squeezed the stuffed bra, the pec.

Christopher gulped and licked his glossy lips, his glowing body quivering. He pitched his voice two octaves higher and gushed, 'Oh, please, mister! I don't want to get hurt.'

Suggs ate it up, groping both pecs, frotting Christopher's ass. 'We'll keep ya in the background, in the dress. I got four other girls dolled up in Arabian harem outfits. They strip down to their G-strings and pasties, but we'll keep ya pure and innocent and clothed. The girl-next-door in a cooch show. The suckers'll shell out for sure.'

Suggs dropped his left hand down to Christopher's groin. He roughly gripped and squeezed the young man's swelling erection, thrashing his tongue around in one of Christopher's shell-like ears. Christopher sighed and arched back against the big man, undulating his pert bottom up against Suggs' erection, squeezing it with his cheeks.

'Yeah!' Suggs groaned. 'We're gonna make ourselves a mint.'

He spun Christopher around in his arms, bear-hugged the dolled youth right up off the floorboards and slammed his mouth into Christopher's. He hungrily kissed him, swarmed his tongue into the blond's pink mouth, scooped up Christopher's butt cheeks with his hands.

Christopher let out a squeal and flung his arms around Suggs's neck, eagerly sucking on the man's thick red tongue.

Suggs rode Christopher up and down his big body, his huge hard-on, with his hands on the feminised youth's ass. Then he carried Christopher over to a battered steel desk. He swept the clutter on top away with a swipe of his arm, plopped Christopher down on the desk, split the dress open, ripped Christopher's panties apart. The young man slumped back against the wall, looking stunned and seductive, eyes hooded and mouth hanging open, hard cock jutting out.

Suggs pulled off his jacket and bowtie and shirt, unfastened and shoved down his pants. His chest was broad and hairy and ridged with muscle. His cock speared out and up from his fiery loins, a butt-plugger of fearsome proportions.

Christopher cupped a pec, pinched and rolled an engorged nipple, running his tongue over his lush lips, twitching his smooth cut cock up and down. Suggs pulled a jar of greasepaint out of a desk drawer and slathered his dong, fingered Christopher's rosebud. The young man squealed, jumped and clutched the thick probing digit deep in his manhole.

'Here she comes, girlie!' Suggs gritted, gripping his prong and boring forward.

Christopher lifted his legs and grasped the back of his thighs, opening up his pink anus. Suggs slammed his bloated cap against the young man's starfish. The beefy hood squished through the erotic opening and the bulging, clenching ass ring. Both men held their breath as Suggs ploughed into Christopher's dainty bottom.

Take Me

Suggs exhaled, gripped Christopher's trembling thighs up against his massive bare chest, jerked the young man forward and fully buried eight torrid inches of vein-pumped cock in Christopher's butt. He pumped his powerful hips, rocking the winsome blond on the end of his sledge. Christopher desperately pulled on his buzzing nipples as his own flapping cock marked the hot, brutal pace of the reaming and flung pre-come, his body and butt burning with raw, wicked pleasure.

'Fuck, Chrissie! Fuck!' Suggs gasped, pumping faster and harder.

Christopher bounced off the wall. Strangled moans and groans and the savage smack of heated flesh against flesh filled the crackling air. Suggs pulled his fingers from Christopher's thigh, grabbed the young man's cock and jacked it in rhythm to his plunging dong.

'Oh, Mr Suggs!' Christopher wailed. 'You're making me come!'

Suggs bellowed and bucked and blasted, his thundering dong exploding in Christopher's anus, searing the blond's insides with jets of semen. Just then a rope of hot sperm leaped out of Christopher's hand-cranked cock, followed by another, and another, and another, striping his dewy torso, basting the boy with utter joy.

* * *

The cooch show went off without a hitch that night. 'Chrissie' was the obvious amateur among the professional girls, shy and awkward and oh, so alluring. The crowd of hicks lapped it up and swallowed it down. They could picture themselves in their own dirty mind's eye really making it with Chrissie, the girl next door, so unlike the other exotic beauties.

And Christopher could picture some of the handsome rubes making it with him, also. Which gave the young man an idea.

The other cooch girls were in on Christopher's act, but the Scarecrow swore them to secrecy. The rest of the men and women in the travelling menagerie didn't have a clue. The bearded lady and the electric girl didn't even deign to talk to just another 'hussy'. But the spielers and card- and dicemen cast appreciative glances Christopher's way, checking out the new talent; and the dog-faced boy and Tom Thumb openly leered.

The circus followed the sun all the way north to Minnesota, Christopher riding in comfort in Suggs's berth, in a style he wasn't used to. The bossman fawned over him, showering him with affection and loving, paying him more than the other cooch girls. Yet, when a guy's got a good thing going, he only wants better.

So when a hick caught the young man all alone and unattended, Christopher decided to put his brewing plans into action.

The man was the mayor of a minor town on the Missouri River. Christopher had seen him at the cooch show every one of their three consecutive days at the stop, and so, when the middle-aged sucker crowded in on him at the back of a tent, Christopher was little surprised and lots of happy.

'I, um, really admire the way you dance, young lady,' the man puffed, his jowly face flushing. 'You've got real talent, let me tell you.'

Christopher saw what the bald-headed man was really admiring – his girlish figure in the strapless, red velvet, body-hugging dress the Scarecrow had stitched together. He knew his turn on the stage would never land him a leading role in any Ziegfeld Follies. But he murmured, 'Why, thank you,' casting his blue eyes demurely downwards.

The man jerked a ham-hand off the lapel of his suit coat and brushed puffy fingers up and down Christopher's bare right arm. Christopher trembled with feigned nervousness, and delight.

The mayor's seduction was as awkward as the sword-swallower's speech. He stammered and stumbled, fumbled with Christopher. Until he finally paid the young man dolled up as a woman the ultimate compliment Christopher was looking for – a ten-dollar bill in a shaking mitt.

'You – you remind me of my daughter – 's best friend.'

Christopher tucked the fresh sawbuck into his manmade cleavage, swooned down to his knees in the grass and pulled the man's cock out and into his wet-velvet mouth.

It was the quickest and easiest ten bucks he'd ever earned. Unlike the 'bos on the rails, these hicks were more than willing to pay for it.

Christopher turned it into a business, giving the eye to an ogling prospect and then meeting him after the show in some secluded tent fold or out back in the bushes, giving the rube the blowjob of his lewd dreams. Suck for the suckers.

Christopher's grouchbag grew lettuce. And since Suggs and the Scarecrow didn't know what he was up to, he didn't have to cut them in for a dime.

And when the Scarecrow was showing off her new camera one day, Christopher got an even better idea for really cashing in before the circus and the cooch show folded up in the fall.

They were working the outskirts of Fargo, North Dakota. Christopher had cased out an abandoned shack in a neighbouring farmer's field. And the first night there, he led the West Fargo sheriff out to the shack by the hand.

He'd rigged the Scarecrow's camera with a long string, so that when he was flat on his back on a rickety table, and the sheriff had just porked his anus with cock (because Chrissie 'didn't want to get pregnant'), he pulled his covering panties all the way aside and pulled on the string.

172

The camera flash stunned the lawman. But not so much as the sight of Christopher's penis. He didn't know what was happening, couldn't figure it out. Until it all became clear a couple of days later, when he received a letter from Christopher with a copy of the photograph of him buried balls-deep in a man's ass.

The hush money came by return post, to the next circus stop in the neighbouring state. Blackmail was never so easy, so profitable, so pleasurable. Christopher was on his way.

He ran the sting all the way out west – enticing prominent citizens to hit on him, hammer into him, before he pulled the panty curtain to reveal his masculinity and tripped the light fantastic to catch the badgers in his game. His grouchbag bulged.

He was making exotic plans for the winter, when the Superintendent of Schools of Missoula, Montana stuck his swollen cock into Christopher's rectum and urgently banged away – just as Suggs and the Scarecrow busted into the broken-down barn.

'Been workin' for yourself, huh?' Suggs growled, striding up to the pair *in flagrante delicto*.

'What–what's going on here?' the educator bleated.

'Get your dick outta that boy and take a powder, rube!' the Scarecrow hissed.

Suggs ripped Christopher's panties to the side, exposing the young man's semi-erection. Christopher felt the superintendent's cock shrivel inside him. The Scarecrow helped shoot the stunned man through the barn doors and back into the night.

Suggs grabbed Christopher's grouchbag, then hauled the young man up by the scruff of his dress and shook him. 'Your circus days are over, sweetheart!' he snarled. 'Nobody runs a game in my outfit without cuttin' me in!'

'Little slut!' the Scarecrow screeched, showing her claws.

Christopher had screwed around, and now he was getting the 'set-straight'.

But just as Suggs and the Scarecrow had begun bouncing the blond off the barn walls, the door suddenly crashed open with a bang. 'Get yer dirty mitts off'n that little girl!' the strongman roared.

The trio gaped at him. They'd never heard the shy, soft-spoken, gentle giant utter an angry sentence before. He was dressed in his leopard-skin tights, muscles bulging all over his bare chest and arms, shaven head gleaming menacingly in the light of the hurricane lamp.

'Blow, Louis!' Suggs rasped, not letting go of Christopher. 'This don't concern you!' He turned back to the blond and slapped him hard across his pretty, made-up face.

One second Christopher was hanging in midair with a stinging cheek. The next second he was stretched out on his back in the hay, resting comfortably, watching as

Louis grabbed Suggs and the Scarecrow by their scruffy necks and slammed their scheming heads together. The hollow crack echoed through the barn.

Louis tossed the unconscious pair outside like two sacks of manure.

Then the strongman bent down next to Christopher, his dark eyes soft behind his bushy brows. 'We're leavin' this crummy road show,' he said. 'You an' me. I–I been in love with ya first time I saw ya.' He reached out a platter-sized palm and cupped Christopher's slapped cheek and that side of the young man's blond head.

Christopher smiled at the giant's gentle touch, blinking tears out of his big blue eyes. He snuck a hand under his dress and made sure his panties were back covering his unmentionables. Then he kissed his hero on the man's thick, soft lips.

Louis crushed Christopher to his massive chest, his mouth locked on Christopher's mouth, lips moving. Christopher coiled his arms around the strongman's corded neck and embraced and kissed him back.

Louis rolled over onto his back in the hay, man and 'girl' hugging tight. Christopher darted his tongue into Louis's mouth, flicking it against the giant's huge licker. He shot a hand down in between them and grabbed onto Louis's cock in his tights, stroking the enormous erection. Louis groaned from deep in his big body, his shovel-hands engulfing Christopher's butt cheeks.

175

Christopher squirmed lower on the man. He pulled the strap off Louis's right shoulder, fully exposing the giant's hairy chest and hard pink nipples. They were like twin gum drops. Christopher licked them, teasing them harder still with his swirling pink tongue. Louis almost bucked the young man right up into the air with his joy, his cock pulsating in Christopher's shifting hand like an electric cable.

Christopher popped up onto the man's tree-trunk thighs and pulled Louis's tights all the way down. The giant's dong sprang free and speared out over his muscle-banded stomach. Christopher bent his head down and kissed the tremendous erection, licked it, lifted it up, stuck the huge purpled cap into his mouth and sucked on it.

'Yeah, baby!' Louis groaned, clutching handfuls of hay, his eyes rolling back in his head.

Christopher sucked up maybe half of the throbbing, wrist-thick pink dong. It bulged his cheeks and bloated his throat. He bobbed his blond-wigged head up and down, sucking tight and wet, cupping and squeezing the giant's great hairy balls.

Until a spurt of pre-come salted his throat.

Christopher disgorged the mammoth erection and rose up on his knees again. He plucked a jar of greasepaint out of the hay and lubed Louis's cock and his own frightened and excited starfish. Then he hiked up his dress and pulled his panties aside at the back, careful to keep his cock covered, stuck the giant's hammerhead in between his quivering cheeks and sat back.

Louis's hood punched into Christopher's ass. The young man saw stars, felt bliss, as he impaled himself on the pink spike, inches and inches of shaft stuffing and splitting his anus.

Christopher's bum touched down onto Louis's thighs, the man's huge cock fully buried inside. They both moaned. Christopher planted his small, sweating hands on the giant's heaving chest and undulated his bum, bouncing up and down, fucking himself on Louis's cock.

Louis's eyes popped open like his gaping mouth and he grabbed Christopher's slim waist, pumped his hips, thrusting his pipe back and forth in Christopher's chute. The pair shimmered like the midway lit up at showtime.

Louis bucked Christopher up into the air with the force of his lusty thrusting, his sawing cock sending the young man sailing. And Christopher's cock sprang free from his wrenched panties to flap up and down right in front of them, keeping pace with the frantic butt-fucking. Christopher stared down at his bared, bouncing erection, at Louis's face. But Louis just grinned and pumped harder, faster, reaming Christopher's ass in a passionate frenzy.

'Yes, Louis! Oh, yes!' Christopher cried, catapulted to the heights of sheer ecstasy by the surging, searing stroke of the strongman's cock. His own cock spurted out his joy all on its own, striping Louis's chest.

Just as Louis grunted and shuddered and shot torrents of hot come splashing against Christopher's bowels.

The giant held Christopher in his brawny arms afterwards, making plans for the both of them.

'And–and you don't mind that I'm a –'

'That yer a girl with a boy's … tool?' Louis squeezed Christopher tight. 'Naw! I been around freaks too long to worry 'bout somethin' like that. I love ya, Chrissie.'

Someone that dumb deserved to be taken, Christopher thought, emotionally and financially. That's the law of the road show: never give a sucker an even break.

So, while the strongman dozed, Christopher relieved him of his grouchbag. Then he picked the bossman and the Scarecrow clean as they slept off their concussions.

With that haul, the young man's road days were over. For a good long while, anyway.

Printed in Great Britain
by Amazon